About the author

John T. Leonard is a pseudonym. At the time of first publication the author was a serving Police Officer, and he feels a certain anonymity is essential given the content of this story, as well as his previous and future projects.

Primus was Leonard's second project. His first project, *Settling The Score* was a semi-autobiographical story of an injured Police Officer seeking retribution. This story was written whilst the author was himself recovering from surgery but not as a result of any assault received in the course of his work.

The author was born and raised in South East England. He is a divorced father of two young children. He currently resides south of London.

By his own admission he does suffer with his mental health, specifically anxiety, and as a result is an advocate for anyone who suffers similarly.

John T Leonard can be contacted directly at jtlnovels@gmail.com

PRIMUS

John T Leonard

PRIMUS

Vanguard Press

VANGUARD PAPERBACK

© Copyright 2019
John T Leonard

The right of John T Leonard to be identified as author of
this work has been asserted by him in accordance with the
Copyright, Designs and Patents Act 1988.

A CIP catalogue record for this title is
available from the British Library.

ISBN 978 1 784655 43 3

*Vanguard Press is an imprint of
Pegasus Elliot MacKenzie Publishers Ltd.*
www.pegasuspublishers.com

First Published in 2019

**Vanguard Press
Sheraton House Castle Park
Cambridge England**

Printed & Bound in Great Britain

Dedication

This book is dedicated to my parents, the real heroes of my story, for without whose love and support, this release would never have been realised.

FOREWORD

A child comes into the world with a handful of selves which are only loosely integrated. Normally, throughout childhood, integration of the selves increases, then during adolescence the child's *corporate self* is represented by a now unified system comprising of parallel streams of consciousness.

However, as a result of emotional trauma in an inescapable environment, delivering to the subject horrible memories, there is a disruption in this normal system of integration, which can result in several outcomes.

Some *selves* can then fail to integrate with the *corporate self*. These *selves* then form the alternative personalities of Dissociative Identity Disorder (DID). This will not be true for all *selves*. Some *selves* will again integrate with each other and these will form what is commonly called the 'host', 'original' or 'core' personality in DID.

Alternative personalities will 'leave' the *Realm Primus*, escaping, for a time the reality of the subject's situation, to inhabit another *realm* (a *mindscape*). Some of these alters will go into *hibernation* and sleep for, perhaps, years – or may never reawaken.

Day 1

"Grab your coat, Tom, we've been given a body," a voice yelled from across the office.

Detective Sergeant Tom Draven put down his coffee and peered over the top of his computer monitor in the direction of where the voice had come from.

He took off his glasses and rubbed his eyes. He looked at his watch, it was early, it was 8:47 a.m., but he had already been at his desk for nearly two hours. Despite the reason for the excursion he smiled at the notion of having an excuse to get out of the office. He locked his computer and stood up. He pushed his chair in, then took his jacket from the back of it and gracefully slid one arm, then the other, into the sleeves before straightening the collar.

He looked across the office to see that his colleague Detective Constable Carl Wainwright had now sat back down at his desk.

Enough time to finish my coffee then, he thought.

Still standing, he picked up his mug and looked across at his colleague in such a way as if to say *hurry up* to Wainwright who seemed to have already forgotten the urgency he was apparently trying to instil in Draven.

As Draven was the senior officer, he was leaving the matter of collating reports and collecting an investigation log and a *go-bag* to Carl.

A *go-bag* was essentially a bag of any kind, usually a sports holdall which had police officer evidence bags, plastic tubes for the collection of knives, as well as other items for the documentation, seizure and preservation of evidence from a crime scene.

They could both expect that uniformed officers would already be on the scene they were about to attend, but from experience, it never hurt to have *too* many evidence bags.

"I'm just printing off the CAD report," Carl said, explaining the reason he was delaying their departure.

The CAD report, or *Computer Aided Dispatch* report, is a chronological log that is created following first contact regarding an incident. This could be initiated by a call from a member of the public or by an officer themselves. This provides an indelible date/time stamped log of entries made.

Tom now had time to tidy up a bit. He didn't like a cluttered desk, he felt it reflected badly on him. He picked his glasses up, folded the arms in and placed them into the case which was on his desk. Tom only needed to wear glasses for close work, for reading and computer use. He left this pair at work as he had a second pair at home.

With his desk in a state that he was prepared to leave it in he was now ready. He looked over at Carl, who he could see was now also ready.

They both headed across the office towards the door that exited the offices for the Serious Crimes Unit (SCU).

The department itself looked like any normal commercial or business office. All of the personnel who worked there were either plain-clothed police officers or civilian investigators.

It appeared normal, except for the fact that the windows were tinted by an adhesive film to make them into a two-way mirror. This was because the walls were covered with the sort of images that would make the most hardened soul feel queasy. Also, amongst these abhorrent images, were posters for the persons wanted in connection with current investigations.

The mirrored film on the windows was designed to prevent anyone using one of the tower blocks of flats across the road from the police station being given an elevated position to then be able to use a long lens and spy on the goings-on in the office, or view any of the evidence or confidential information on display.

Amongst the images and *wanted* posters were intelligence reports and also affixed to the walls were crime scene photos including before and after pictures of victims.

They weren't all murder victims though, the SCU itself was sub-divided into teams dealing with different offences that were all deemed as being serious crimes. These teams were clustered and identified by signs hanging from the ceiling above their desk denoting their area of specialism: ROBBERY, FRAUD, OCG, SEX OFF, and MURDER. Offences deemed not to be serious were dealt with by a detective in the Criminal Investigation Department (CID).

Both Tom and Carl had started working for the police as uniformed officers, dealing with responding to 999 calls and low-level investigations before transferring to CID, and ultimately being seconded to the SCU.

They were the only two officers working the murder team that day, and it was evident from the smile on his face that Carl shared Tom's sentiment that at the very least he saw the report of a body being found as an excuse to get out of the office for a couple of hours.

"Fancy a quick puff before we head off?" Carl said to Tom as they stepped outside.

This was met with a scornful look from Tom. Carl thought it wise not to say anything further on the subject. Carl knew full well that Tom was yet again in the process of quitting smoking, and from the look he gave Carl he didn't appreciate his colleague's attempts to scupper his efforts.

oOo

Whereas the teams that responded to 999 calls and dealt with neighbourhood issues were split into divisions, the SCU covered the entire county. This meant that, on occasion, the journey from their base station to the incident scene was invariably a long one. Today was no different, but this at least gave Tom and Carl sufficient time to review the CAD log.

As the two of them drove to the scene they were able to get up to speed with what was known so far. Carl drove, and Tom reviewed the log.

He muttered isolated facts as he read them:

"Time of call 0637 hrs."

"Informant was a dog walker, body found just off a well-used track."

"Body is of a white male, possibly in his twenties, no ID as yet."

"COD unknown."

COD refers to cause of death. Although the official cause is determined by the coroner, circumstantial evidence at the scene can give an indication, for instance in the course of a hanging, the logical explanation for the cause of death would be strangulation or asphyxiation, and should the body be recovered from water then drowning could very well be a fair assumption. However, this was only ever an indication, and never taken as gospel. Just as a hanging shouldn't be flippantly dismissed as a suicide just because the hands aren't found to be bound.

"Body was found away from the track, slumped against a tree, drug needles and other paraphernalia found nearby. Hmmm, could well be a self-inflicted overdose, but it's still considered sus' at this time."

The journey to the scene took the best part of an hour. It wasn't *that* far from the police station, but they were now catching the tail end of the morning rush hour and school run which led to inevitable delays.

Their brief for the incident took a matter of minutes as the incident log had limited information on it.

Although Tom was Carl's supervisor and line manager they had worked together for some time, and when out of the office the usual decorum and respect reserved when addressing an officer of a senior rank was left behind.

"How's things with Jess then, seen her recently?" Carl asked.

The delay before replying was so long that Carl was about to ask for a second time, thinking his first attempt hadn't been heard.

"Things are a little sticky at the mo, missed another date."

Carl had started to smirk at the thought of something *sticky* and had been concocting a smutty reply until he thought better of it.

"Oh, what happened?" he finally resorted to asking.

"We had something set up the other evening, but I must've completely forgotten about it. The day came and went, and I didn't even notice. Left her stood up at the movies. She called me up the following day and gave me a right arse chewing. I just had to bullshit her a bit saying a job had come, that I was paged and that I had to attend. I didn't like having to lie to her but somehow I completely lost an entire day."

He looked over and saw Carl shaking his head giving a sympathetic, yet patronising look. "I know, I know," Tom said, agreeing with Carl's sentiment.

"I think I've smoothed things over, we've rescheduled it for another day, I'm just glad it was just a movie and I didn't leave her sat alone at a restaurant. The strangest thing was there were missed calls on my phone, and a voicemail, and I didn't do anything about it, I didn't know anything about it."

Carl was puzzled by this explanation and was about verbalise a response when his phone rang. He took it from his jacket and saw it was a call he had to take.

As Carl was otherwise engaged, Tom sat in quiet contemplation, trying to figure out the chain of events that caused him to forget their date as they had planned.

As they turned the corner into the road that led up to the track off which the body was discovered, they found themselves passing a row of parked police cars. Beyond that was parked a mobile incident unit which was essentially nothing more than a converted minibus, and then an unmarked van that the Scenes of Crimes Officers (SoCO) used.

Once they had parked themselves, there was no mistaking where they needed to go.

The road itself was a dead end. It was a residential road that ended with en-block garages on either side, beyond that it led into the unmade track itself.

DS Tom Draven and DC Carl Wainwright approached a uniformed police officer who had been designated as log-keeper on the scene guard outer cordon. The cordon itself was indicated by a line of blue and white POLICE LINE DO NOT CROSS barrier tape.

They were required to be booked into the log: giving their name, rank, and warrant numbers to the log-keeper.

Tom asked the log-keeper for a brief update as to what had taken place since police had first arrived on the scene.

It transpired that police had been on scene for almost three hours. The first officer to attend had liaised directly with the dog walker who had discovered the body.

The unmade track had since been closed at both ends which formed the outer cordon, and an inner cordon established around the actual location where the body was found.

Tom also looked at the log to see how many people, police officers and forensic staff had been admitted into the scene.

Prior to his and Carl's names being added to the log, only the officers on scene when the log was started, their supervisor and the forensics team had been added.

The dog walker who had discovered the body had since left to go home. They were accompanied by an officer whose intention was to get a written account from them, and to deal with any ongoing welfare issues as a result of having made such a ghastly discovery. "Have you had to turn many people away since you've been here?" Tom asked.

The officer closed the log book and counted up the hash marks he'd made on the front cover.

"Seven, eight, nine. Nine in total, all dog walkers. It's not a cut-through to anywhere."

Tom thanked the log-keeper as he and Carl ducked under the blue and white barrier tape.

"Stick to the left, the common approach is to the left," the officer added, "they're all about two hundred yards up, just beyond where you can see now."

"What's beyond that, where does this path lead?" Tom asked, as he was not overly familiar with this area.

The officer was prepared for this question. He had a ring-bound A-Z atlas already opened at the right page showing the wider area.

"We're here," the officer said pointing to the map. "The track is maybe three-quarters of a mile long, they're all here before the path splits," he continued, tracing his fingers across the page.

"This is all dense woodland," he said circling his finger around where the body was found, "and then it opens up into fields here."

Tom thanked him again.

They looked up the track in front of them. It was a narrow, relatively straight track. It was wide enough for a car, but nothing bigger.

Although the track was wide enough for a car they walked in single file along the left side of the path as instructed.

A *common approach path* is determined as being an illogical approach route to the scene. This is used to avoid trampling any possible forensics evidence along the way when in haste to get to the scene itself. This may include tyre tracks, footprints or anything brought to the scene and discarded whether intentionally or accidentally.

As they walked the common approach path along the left side of the track they could see small yellow triangular markers that had been placed by the SoCO at irregular intervals, at things that may be of interest. Tom paused as they passed each one. Sometimes the reason for its placement was immediately apparent, other times less so, and after failed scrutiny they moved on.

The first one was placed near to where muddy tyre tracks had continued from the unmade track onto the asphalt leaving a distinct tread pattern in raised mud. Another was placed near to a partial shoe print with a fairly distinct tread pattern.

It's certainly not a Reebok Classic, Tom thought.

The Reebok Classic was statistically proven to be the most commonly catalogued shoe print from crime scenes for a number of years. This print, however, appeared to be from a work boot of some kind.

As they continued up the track they rounded a gentle bend. Ahead of them they saw more barrier tape, similar to that passed before, though this was red and white and denoted the inner cordon. Here they could see a couple more uniformed officers and the SoCOs in their white forensic suits.

Tom paused, he looked back towards the road, beyond where the PC stood by the outer cordon. It became apparent that it was now impossible to see the road from where he now stood. He was probably at the minimum distance up the track that facilitated this.

Tom saw Carl scribble a quick note in his investigation log to reflect this observation.

As they continued towards the inner cordon they could see the familiar shape of a white forensics tent. It looked completely out of place in the woodland ahead. The stark white of the tent contrasted heavily against the natural colours of its surroundings.

All the trees in this wood appeared to be evergreen, thus ensuring the foliage was dense all year round.

They approached the inner cordon barrier tape getting the attention of another uniformed police officer standing there.

Tom stopped again. He looked back down the track towards the road. The road was now very much out of sight from where they stood. If not due to the distance and terrain, it was due to the foliage.

He listened. Aside from the activity going on behind them, it was silent. Tom looked at his watch, it was mid-morning now, meaning it was even quieter three hours ago.

"Whatever happened here, it's a perfect location for it to happen," he said to Carl who nodded. They were both in agreement that this location was chosen to afford the perpetrator maximum privacy in his deed.

They then looked towards the uniformed officer on the inner cordon. "Morning," the officer said as he lifted the barrier tape for them both to duck under. They said their thanks in unison.

Tom and Carl were now standing inside the inner cordon. Tom was a detective sergeant and had been for many years, but he knew his place when it came to this phase of the investigation.

The Senior SoCO had overall authority over the crime scene at this moment in time. Any unauthorised actions by either Tom or Carl could disturb or destroy any forensic evidence at the scene and potentially scupper any future investigation.

That was the reason for the common approach path, and it was also the reason that they waited patiently for a SoCO to approach them or invite them over to view the scene.

They didn't have to wait long before a SoCO approached them. She introduced herself and gave them a brief update of what had taken place since their involvement.

"We've got an as yet unidentified male, approximately twenty to twenty-five years of age. You can see him leaning against a tree just through there," she then paused to point in the direction of the tent. The flaps which formed the doors were tied back showing what she was describing.

"We only have one set of shoe prints going to and from the body, same tread pattern. The *to* prints are distinctly deeper than the *from* prints suggesting that the body was carried to this location, or at the very least from the path."

She paused having seen Carl scribbling more notes in his log. When he looked up, she continued.

"There are fresh puncture wounds to the body. The left arm isn't in its sleeve. It's either a new drug habit or foul play as there aren't any historic needle marks on either arm."

"Can we come over yet?" Carl asked.

"Hold on a sec, I'll ask," she replied, then walked back towards the tent. Her voice was muffled as she was speaking through a face mask similar in appearance to that of a surgeon.

When she returned she was carrying two pairs of plastic overshoes. They look like undersized shower caps, which slip over existing footwear. They have the word *POLICE* moulded into the tread, so the pattern is distinct and can readily be identified and eliminated at any scene. She handed the overshoes to the detectives and watched in amusement as they hopped on one foot then the other as they tried to put them on whilst maintaining some thread of dignity. Having enjoyed the spectacle, she felt the need to add a comment.

"Y'know, it would've been a lot easier for one of you to put them on whilst leaning on the other, then switch over, just saying. Follow me."

Neither Tom nor Carl could see the lower half of her face as it was covered by the face mask but given the sarcasm in her voice, they were confident that she must've been smiling at them. Then came a condescending head tilt. Then when Tom and

Carl looked at her wide-eyed, and feeling suitably chastised, they noticed a protruding bulge coming from the middle of the face mask where her mouth would be. The SoCO was sticking her tongue out at them.

She then turned and walked a very specific and now well-trodden route between the path and the tent. Much like the defined route along the path, it was outside of the area that had been determined to have been used during the incident.

Tom chuckled to himself at the amusement their earlier spectacle caused as they both walked behind the SoCO. As they approached the forensics tent they each pulled on a pair of purple latex examination gloves. Carl found this to be awkward as he held his pen in his teeth and his log book under his arm.

The SoCO pointed out the footprints leading to and from the tent which were again marked with the yellow numbered triangular markers. As she pointed at them, another SoCO who was in the process of photographing each shoe print stopped what she was doing and stood back to allow her colleague to make her point. "Size eight," she said. This was again slightly muffled as she was speaking through a face mask.

Carl didn't feel the need to document this as a full forensics report would be forthcoming which would contain all these details as well as the photographs that were being taken.

As they viewed the various shoe prints they could see that the ones to the body were indeed distinctly deeper than those leaving it.

The SoCO led them to the open entrance to the tent and left them there. She then went back to her previous task. Tom and Carl turned to watch her leave. Tom was adamant he could see her shoulders judder as if she was chuckling. Perhaps continuing to regale in his earlier exploits. He thought it wasn't *that* funny, but it must've been a slow day.

They were standing there for a matter of seconds when another SoCO, one who had previously been crouched beside the body, beckoned them over to join him. He indicated with a pointed finger the route they should take towards him.

As they approached he stood up and pulled down his face mask to address them both.

They both knew him to be the Senior SoCO.

"Morning Dave," Tom said, "what have we got here then?"

"Good morning Tom, Carl, how are you?" came the reply.

"All good here," Tom replied. Carl just smiled and nodded.

"What we've got here is an unidentified male with no obvious physical signs of injury. Found as you see him. Left arm out of his sleeve, puncture wounds, drug paraphernalia strewn around him suggesting usage. One set of shoe prints in, one set out, neither of them his."

Tom looked back towards where the uniformed officer stood on the path. He estimated he was about ten to fifteen yards away.

"Well he certainly didn't jump this far," said Tom.

Tom looked back at the body. He was precariously propped up against the tree, slumped over to his right side. It would only take a gentle breeze to blow him over.

The paraphernalia which the incident log and SoCO had referred to was nothing more than a single hypodermic needle which had been discarded within arm's reach of the body. The plunger was down, but there was residue inside it suggesting it had been used.

The deceased was a young man, clean shaven and once fresh-faced, with fair cropped hair. His blue eyes were still open, staring back towards the path.

Had he been alive to see his killer leave? Tom thought.

"There's nothing in any of his pockets," Dave added.

Tom could hear Carl on the phone to Police Control making enquiries about any missing person reports where the subject matched the description of the poor wretch sat so pathetically in front of them.

"He's definitely been carried to this spot I'd say," Tom said, "the question being – was he dead or alive when he was brought here?"

Carl re-joined the conversation having ended his call to Control. "There's no matching misper reports for us or on PNC."

Misper is an abbreviated term for a missing person, of which there are markers held on the Police National Computer (PNC).

"Any idea how long he's been here?" Carl asked.

"Well the body is in full rigor, so we're looking at least four hours in this climate and how he's dressed. He had a liver temperature of twenty-nine point seven degrees at nine o'clock, which again suggests he'd been here about five hours prior to that," Dave replied.

Carl scribbled these figures down. He looked at his watch. "So, we're looking at about four a.m. for the dump then?"

"That is on the proviso that he was dead when he was left here," Tom added.

The formula used to determine the time of death equates to the body temperature, which is normally at 37.5°C, typically losing 1.5°C per hour until the temperature of the body is that of the environment around it, also known as the ambient temperature. This ambient temperature, depending on how low it is, may take minutes or hours to be reached, however, this is a good preliminary indicator of how long a body has been in situ.

The most common way of taking the temperature of the deceased is to use a rectal thermometer, or to take a temperature reading from the liver, which can achieve a more accurate core body temperature.

Rigor mortis also acts as a good measuring stick for estimating the time of death. This natural process occurs when a body dies, by way of the natural contracting and relaxation of the body's muscles caused by changes in the body's chemical balances. Rigor normally occurs in the smaller muscles such as those in the face and neck and will work its way down through the body to the larger muscles. The process normally begins roughly two hours after death and can last for anything from twenty to thirty hours. Rigor is one of the most common ways of estimating death as it occurs in the body during the first thirty-six to forty-eight hours. However, because there are so many factors that can affect it, using the body temperature is more accurate.

"How much more have you guys got to do here?" Tom asked Dave.

"We're pretty much done with the body, then it'll just be a case of getting plaster casts of the shoe prints and working our way back to the road," Dave replied.

"OK, well, feel free to get the body removed whenever you're ready," Tom said. "When do you think you'll have the preliminary report to me by?"

"Give me a couple of days for the scene and photographs."

"Fab. What happened here?" Tom asked rhetorically.

"That's not my job, that's yours, mate," Dave replied.

oOo

Tom and Carl discussed their findings on the way back to the police station.

They were now waiting on the forensics report as well as the report from the coroner, and they still had to identify their victim.

All they were able to deduce so far was that there was someone else involved, and that someone had possibly carried the victim to the location and left him against the tree, then left as they had presumably arrived.

Since returning to the station the incident report had been updated with the results of the *house-to-house* enquires that uniformed officers had been carrying out. So far no one who lived locally that had been spoken to had seen or heard anything that night. Calling cards were left at all houses that didn't answer with the hope that if they had anything of interest then they would then call in. The police simply didn't have the resources to keep calling at an address over and over in the hope that someone there might have something to add.

Also, the statement provided by the dog walker who had discovered the body didn't reveal anything. His dog had run off the lead and when he failed to return when called, the owner then followed the dog into the shrubbery and made the gruesome discovery, which he immediately called in to the police, and then remained there until the first officer arrived.

According to the temperature of the body, it had been there for several hours before being discovered too. No one in their right mind would be walking that path at that time of night. With dense shrubbery and no street lighting, the scene would most likely have been in pitch blackness when the body was brought there.

Carl had a note scribbled in his log to make contact with the local milk delivery company on the off-chance that they may have seen something. Essentially, they had to be seen to kick over all the stones they could, so they wouldn't be criticised should the investigation come up against a dead end.

"I don't think there's anything more we can do today, tomorrow's gonna probably be a long day *if* we get the reports in. Get yourself off home and enjoy your evening okay. I'll see you tomorrow," Tom said to Carl.

"I'm certainly not going to argue with that," he replied, already in the process of logging off his computer and tidying his desk. "I'll see you tomorrow then."

There wasn't anything more for Tom to do either. He didn't have to report his departure to anyone as it was just the two of them in. He logged off his computer too, then collected the CAD report, the investigation log and the photocopied notes he'd taken from Carl and left the office. It was significantly before the end of his shift, so he quietly left the office without saying goodbye to anyone as he didn't want to advertise to everyone that he and Carl had left early.

oOo

Tom lived alone. Although Jess was his long-term girlfriend they had never discussed moving in together.

As he had earlier mentioned to Carl things had gone a little off the rails recently: a date had been missed and promises broken. But despite that shortly after he got home his phone buzzed. He had a text that read: *Saw a press release, wanna talk about it?*

He messaged back: *Fancy a chat?* Within seconds his phone rang.

Tom answered and spent the next thirty-seven minutes chatting to Jess. Despite the recent friction between them he still wasn't being very attentive. His mind was elsewhere.

After the first few minutes of the call, he had put Jess on speakerphone and put his handset down on the table in front of him. As he distantly spoke to her he was flicking through Carl's notes and reviewing the incident log.

His mind came back to the conversation before the end, just in time to have a conscious agreement to meet Jess for a coffee in a couple of days. He scribbled the day and time onto the photocopied notes before saying his goodbyes and hanging up.

Coffee Jess Thurs 1pm

After he had ended the call, Tom added the date to his phone's calendar. By his own admission, he had a memory like a sieve and had to set alerts on his phone for everything.

Despite this, he had still missed their last date, and for the life of him, he couldn't remember how or why. That date had a reminder set on his phone, but for some unknown reason, that day had completely passed him by.

He loved Jess, they'd been together for over a year. He didn't like knowing that he was the cause of her upset and frustration. He certainly didn't like having to tell a little white lie to save face at having missed their last date.

He had been called into work at a moment's notice whilst off duty before, it's an accepted consequence that came with his rank. So, it was a legitimate excuse for missing the date as it happened. But without it he had no excuse, he couldn't even explain to himself why he had missed it.

Looking back at the notes and investigation log strewn across his table he again drew the conclusion that he could do nothing more without the forensic and coroner's reports, especially as he didn't know who this poor lad was. So, he couldn't even look into his background and any history that the police were aware of.

He tidied away the papers and put his feet up for the remainder of the evening. He knew from experience to enjoy the calm before the storm.

DAY 3

"I saw you in town last night, I did say *hi* but either you didn't hear me, or you were engrossed elsewhere coz you totally blanked me," Carl said as he set a coffee down on the edge of Tom's desk.

Tom paused before offering a response, as he was still trying to make sense of what was just said to him.

"Yesterday?" he questioned. "I didn't go into town yesterday, matter of fact, I haven't been anywhere near town, not off-duty anyway."

"Well, I'm one hundred percent sure it was you, you were even wearing the very same jacket that's on the back of your chair right now," Carl said with a smug look of satisfaction on his face.

Tom continued to look confused, before resigning himself to the fact that he wasn't going to be able to prove Carl wrong. "Well, maybe it's my doppelgänger, *or* they've finally perfected cloning," he joked, just to allow the conversation to move onto more pressing topics.

Tom had his emails open, he had clicked on a message from the forensics team. He hovered over the attachment, and selected the *PRINT* option, he then did the same for the coroner's report.

Tom preferred to view paper files as opposed to scrolling up and down when viewing the same document on the PC monitor. He liked to spread the pages out on the desk, then to highlight relevant points and to be able to scan across multiple pages at the same time. He felt this was by far the best and easiest way to see patterns forming or linking details.

There wouldn't be any patterns forming as a result of these reports, however. In this exercise, it was more a case of finding out exactly what had happened. Tom was hoping to at least have a name for their victim by the end of the shift.

Tom momentarily left Carl sipping his coffee whilst still perched on the corner of his desk to go to the printer to collect his reports. They weren't there waiting for him because the print would only start when the requesting person logged on to the printer, in this case with a swipe card, and selecting the option to print.

The printer whirred into life and started printing Tom's reports. He knew it would take a while to print everything. He wasn't prepared to wait, so he went back to his desk.

As he returned to his desk he himself perched where Carl had previously been, as Carl was now sitting at his own desk.

"Nah, it definitely wasn't me yesterday," Tom said adamantly, referring back to Carl's earlier comment about seeing him in the town the previous day.

Carl looked at him and shrugged his shoulders, as if the topic no longer had any relevance for him.

Maybe it didn't retain any interest to Carl, but it continued to concern and confuse Tom.

After taking a couple more sips of his coffee Carl went over to the printer and waited for the last of Tom's reports to print off.

Tom had printed the reports single-sided. This was so he could spread the sheets out over the desk without anything on the backs being hidden from his gaze. The force occasionally made requests to print double-sided wherever possible to save on stationery, but Tom felt he had a valid reason for his choice.

Carl had a queue behind him at the printer from other officers whose print requests were stacked behind Tom's lengthy reports. "Sorry," was all Carl could say to them, even though the reason for the delay did not lie with him.

The two reports totalled about fifty pages. Carl scanned through the pages like a flicker book as he walked back to his desk.

Carl set them down on Tom's desk. Their desks sat facing each other, with a spare one on the end, which wasn't occupied. But this served as a useful area to spread the reports out without cluttering Tom or Carl's workspaces.

Tom scanned through the forensics report first. It contained dozens of photographs taken of the scene. The images started off with wide shots of the garages, then the approach path, and finally of the body itself. Then the images started to focus in on each topic. Finally, the images were of individual items of specific relevance: shoe prints, tyre treads, drug paraphernalia, the position of the body and close-ups of the hands and face. Each of these photos contained at least one yellow triangular marker that he and Carl had seen on the walk to where the body was found. Each marker was numbered and was then cross-referenced to a list explaining its relevance.

He then began to view the coroner's report. This would give a preliminary indication as to how the young lad died as well as any foreign substances in his bloodstream, the contents of his stomach, as well as any trauma to the body. Trauma is a blanket term to describe any bruises, grazes or any other type of injuries to the body.

It all seems to be here, good job, thanks, Dave, Tom thought.

He then closed the report and flipped it over to return to page one, so as to begin over again with a more thorough review.

Tom leant over the reports resting his bodyweight on his left hand. He had his fluorescent yellow highlighter pen ready in his right hand. He saw the first thing he wanted to highlight. He lifted the marker pen to his mouth and held the cap between his teeth before pulling the pen away exposing the nib. The first thing to be highlighted was:

Name of Subject	Callum BURGESS
Date of birth (age)	20/07/1994 (22)

He had the answer to the question he sorely needed. The forensics and coroner's reports could tell him *how* and *when* that death had taken place.

But the question that Tom and Carl had to answer was *why* and most importantly by *whom?*

Having now identified the deceased, this would lead to a number of separate tasks and enquiries. These included first and foremost identifying and informing the next of kin.

On this occasion identifying the next of kin (NOK) was relatively straightforward. A procedural check on the deceased would be to see if there was a record for them on the national police database. This would be primarily to see if they had been reported missing, but also to determine if they were a firearms certificate holder, and if there were any outstanding firearms. Had there been, these would have to be located and seized as well as any firearms certificates.

As it turned out Burgess was not known on the police database as a missing person (misper) or as a firearms certificate holder. He was however known for a number of theft and violence offences dating back almost ten years. But nothing relating to drug use, supply or possession.

How bizarre, Tom thought.

As this was a known offender, Tom then checked his details against the local database. This was a shared system which gave him access to the

43

host force's records as well as that of the neighbouring forces.

Again, Burgess was well known to this multi-force database. He had been involved in numerous offences over the years, with numbers far in excess of those listed nationally. The reason for this was because the national database only contained records of convictions and cautions, whereas the local databases contained details of all the offences he had been associated with, be that as a suspect, victim or witness.

Burgess also had a marker against his name as being an *Organised Crime Group* (OCG) member. This meant he was either a gang member or was part of a criminal hierarchy. An eventual analysis of specific intelligence would determine which. This would need to be done to potentially lead to the *who* and *why*.

Amongst the information on the local database was a list of known associates. This would be anyone that Burgess has been involved with that resulted in police intervention. This could range from someone he had been arrested alongside, or as trivial as another known offender seen in the same car as him at any given time. With both extremes taken into consideration, the list of known associates contained twenty to thirty names.

Tom did a screen print for the list of associates. He left his desk to go to the printer. He returned after a few minutes with the list to see Carl leant over the spare desk perusing the photos that Tom had taken from the file.

"What's the betting that our killer is on this list?" said Tom, holding the list in such a way so that when Carl looked up he could see what Tom was referring to.

There was a pause as Carl realised what the list of names actually was before nodding his agreement. "Good chance," he replied.

Although the forensics report was very detailed, it did not draw any conclusions. As Dave had mentioned at the scene, that was for the detectives to do. All the forensics report contained was facts, nothing more.

Carl was now in the process of compiling a virtual walkthrough with the photographs. This meant putting them in sequential order, not in the order they were taken or exhibited, but rather in the order they would have been viewed by someone who had entered from the road, via the garages and had continued along the track, much as they themselves did the day before yesterday.

He had laid them out like a movie storyboard or comic strip. Starting in the top left corner of the desk were the images of the residential road, then the en-block garages, before entering the footpath which was tarmacked for the first few yards, presumably to use up what was surplus to requirements when the garage area was last resurfaced, before becoming an unmade muddy track.

It was only once on the track that the images started to feature the yellow forensic markers. Firstly, on the surfaced section indicating tyre treads in raised mud, then on the unmade track with various depressions. With each marker, there was a wide-angle image as well as a close-up image to show the relevant detail. To keep the sequence of photos to a minimum Carl placed the close-ups behind the wide angle.

The sequence led the viewer along the track until the forensic markers ended. An image then showed the track disappearing into the distance, as well as one looking back down the track towards the garages which were now completely out of sight. The images then panned to the right, taking overall shots of the wooded area.

From the track, the white tent could just be seen in the distance, and only because it was in stark contrast to the natural colours of the foliage enveloping it.

The camera view then left the track, panning left and right as it advanced on the tent. Once at the tent, images were taken in all directions, covering a full 360 degrees, including back towards the track; again, the track was only distinguishable from the surrounding foliage by the uniformed police officer in his high-visibility tabard standing there. Finally, the images entered the tent and showed wide angle and close-up images of Burgess as well as the ground where he was sitting.

The images of Burgess started with full-length shots, then close-ups of his head from all sides, each limb and close-ups of his hands and feet including the tread pattern on the footwear.

Further pictures were then taken after bags had been sealed around his hands and feet. More images showed the body after it had been placed in a body bag on a gurney. The final images showed the ground underneath where Burgess had been sitting, after his body had been removed.

The reason that bags were sealed over the hands and feet was to retain any foreign bodies that were in contact with the hands and feet at the time it was in situ to prevent them being accidentally dislodged and discarded during transit. Should they become detached during any movement then they would be caught in the bag and would be retained for forensic analysis.

The last shots showed disturbed debris that had fallen from the trees onto the ground, as well as some small items that could've fallen from a pocket. On closer scrutiny, Carl saw that these items included a few coins and some small papers.

Carl set the photographs down and flicked through the rest of the file to the *Seized Property* form. This contained a list of all the items that were retrieved from the location after the body was sealed into the body bag.

Carl scanned down the list:

-coins

-cigarette papers

-rubber band

-hypodermic needle

"Okay, they're Rizlas," Carl said to himself, eliminating them from requiring any further interest or scrutiny.

This wasn't the only Seized Property form within the file. There was another. This one listed the items that were seized from the body and the body bag after its arrival at the Coroners.

-brown shoe (left)

-brown shoe (right)

-black jeans
-black jacket
-green/blue check shirt
-neck chain (yellow metal)
-digital wrist watch
-velcro wallet
-5 keys on split ring
-disposable lighter

The reason the term *yellow metal* is used is because police officers and police staff do not have the training to determine whether or not something is made of a specific metal. As a result, it is not referred to as being gold or any other metal, just described by its colour.

The Seized Property form then went on to list the contents of the wallet which included bank notes and an Oyster card. There was nothing to give immediate identification as to the owner of the wallet. Normally, there would be the expectation of finding bank cards and possibly other identification and membership cards as well as a driver's licence. But there wasn't any of this. The fact that there was cash in the wallet suggested that this wasn't a robbery, but that there wasn't anything to identify the owner led Carl to believe that someone had intentionally taken these items from the wallet to hinder identifying the deceased.

Carl broke away from the spare desk to his own to quickly check the national police database. Burgess was indeed the holder of a substantive UK driver's licence, which underlined his previous notion.

It was then that another thought occurred to him. It was actually quite commonplace to find suspects without any identification on them. This would be an attempt to use someone else's name should they ever be stopped by police. In most cases, the details given would be that of a sibling or a friend who doesn't have a police record, or who isn't currently wanted for anything.

There was nothing amongst the listed property to warrant immediate specific attention.

"Strange that there's no phone," Carl muttered to himself. "Hey, Sarge, there's no phone amongst his stuff."

Tom looked up from his reports to face Carl with a puzzled look on his face. They both knew full well that people are practically surgically attached to their mobile phones these days.

"No ID either," Carl continued, "either he didn't have any when he went out, or someone is deliberately trying to make our job harder."

They both realised that would be something of a setback because an analysis of the phone would give a contact history: a list of calls and messages to and from Burgess. It could also be also be used to trace what mobile phone network masts it had been connected to, giving some indication as to Burgess' whereabouts in the hours before his death.

They knew this, maybe the killer did too, maybe the phone was intentionally taken prior to attending the final location, or taken from the body along with any ID? Or maybe Burgess had intentionally left it somewhere himself? After all, he was a repeat offender and would know that for the majority of offences he had been arrested for previously, his phone would no doubt have been seized into evidence for scrutiny for intelligence purposes.

They had to entertain the notion that the missing phone did suggest a theory that this could, in fact, be a robbery, but the fact that Burgess had cash on him conflicted with that theory.

"A property search of the area was conducted after the body was removed, but it didn't turn up anything," Tom said as he flicked to another page in the forensic report.

A property search was conducted by a police dog unit. It would've only been conducted after the body had been removed as the focus of the search was based on the freshest scent available to the dog.

"Okay, boss, I think I've got this ready for ya now," Carl said.

"Gimme a sec," Tom replied.

Carl scanned the images in sequence, he swapped a couple of images around to allow the sequence to flow more logically. He smiled and nodded, pleased with the result of his efforts.

"Okay, I'm ready, what have you got for me?" Tom said as he stood and moved round to the end desk to stand next to Carl.

Carl noticed Tom rubbing his eyes feverishly. "Why haven't you got your glasses on?" he asked.

"Eh?" Tom replied with a confused look on his face. He looked back at his desk, and there in front his computer monitor was a glasses case.

"Fucking hell," he said as he walked back round to his desk. He opened the case, took out his spectacles and put them on.

For a moment Tom paused, he cursed himself for what had just happened. He knew he wore glasses, so why was he sitting there suffering from strained eyes whilst his salvation sat in a case, inches from him?

Tom moved back to stand next to Carl as he began to talk him through the sequence of events.

Tom viewed each image in turn as the actions were narrated by Carl.

"Okay, we've not got anything in the way of a vehicle. No tyre treads beyond some raised mud ridges, not enough to give a manufacturer or anything, and nothing from the house-to-house enquiries. Nothing of note on the footpath either, partial shoe prints only, differing treads, nothing obviously matching the prints towards the body or the deceased's himself." Carl paused and looked over at Tom. Seeing he was nodding his understanding, Carl continued.

"This is where it gets interesting; there's only *one* set of shoe prints both to *and* from the body, same print pattern, can rule them out being the deceased as the size doesn't match, they're a size eight, Burgess isn't. Shoe print depth is deeper on the approach, suggesting that the body *may* have been carried there. Scene photos, as you can see, don't suggest anything of a struggle taking place. So, if, and it's a big *if*, why would Burgess shoot up at the location, and *if* he did walk there himself, where's his shoe prints? So, my money's on that he was rendered unconscious elsewhere, carried and dumped there, with the intention of making it look like an OD, hence the used needles et cetera dumped near him."

"Why, though? He wasn't a user, at least nothing's on record to say so, unless he's recently taken up the habit, so what the point, what's being said?" Tom added.

"Well as things stand at the mo, we've got nothing at the scene to point us in any direction. The shoe prints are generic prints in mud, no characteristics to narrow it down to a make." Tom paused. "I guess we'll have to wait for the tox report, and any forensics on the clothing. I think we're done for the day. You've got some time owing, so if you want to get yourself home, then feel free."

Carl didn't need to be told twice, he'd worked some long shifts recently and wasn't going to argue over such an offer.

"Enjoy your rest days. Hopefully, we'll have all the reports when we come back," Tom said.

After straightening up, Tom headed home. They now had two days off before they were back on duty.

oOo

When Tom got home he found a message from Jess on his answering machine. This was quite unusual in itself as she hardly ever called his landline number. Tom took his phone out of his pocket to find the battery was dead. This puzzled him, after all he made a point of charging it every night, added to which he had barely looked at it today.

First the eyestrain from not wearing his glasses, now this. Tom realised he was tired but couldn't explain why. He felt he was sleeping well enough but was still tired during the day. This investigation, like those he'd been on before, was destined to keep him awake, but not yet. For now, he had no explanation for his lapses.

Tom listened to the message as he plugged the charger cable into his mobile phone. Again, it was Jess, she was checking up on him, asking him if he was okay, and then asking if they could change the time for their coffee as she now had a dentist appointment. She wanted to push back the coffee until three p.m. Tom nodded at the change of time.

His mobile phone lit up then went through the start-up process. Once it had reached the home page he started to send Jess a text message.

Coffee – 3pm perfect, sorry I missed your call, battery died, see you there xx

oOo

Later that evening as Tom was again reviewing the reports he had brought home, it was finally dawning on him how late it was.

He thought it was about time he should lay on his bed and stare restlessly at his ceiling whilst he pondered the case, and not in the least try to actually fall asleep.

As he lay there he realised he was right, he wasn't going to be falling asleep any time soon.

Day 5

"Have you ever had one of those *Ohmigod* moments? Y'know, when you stick your hand in your pocket expecting to find your keys or your phone and nothing's there?" Tom paused to take a sip of his coffee.

He was meeting Jess for a coffee as per their revised arrangements. They had met at a town centre chain coffee shop. It was a pleasant enough morning, mild, but warm enough for them to choose to sit outside, although in the shade it had a distinctly cool breeze, especially through the pedestrianised funnel where they sat.

"Well, exactly that happened to me this morning. Went out to the car park to get into my car to come here, and it wasn't there. I thought *Oh fuck, someone's nicked it.* I had a panicked scout around but couldn't see anything. Then it was only by sheer chance that I pressed the button on the remote to see the headlights flash. It was obscured by a van, but it was there. Not where I remember leaving it, that's for sure. I mean I have an allocated bay, so why the hell was it parked in one of the visitors' bays?"

Jess didn't seem the least bit concerned, and it felt as if Tom had given the story as a witty anecdote and not something he was genuinely concerned about.

"I know that feeling, it's horrible when that happens, all's well that ends well though," she replied.

"I'm finding stuff like this is happening more and more often recently. Mainly it's just small stuff like not finding my keys where I think I've left them, only to find them in a coat pocket or somewhere. It's getting to be a habit, but it's a right pain in the arse; if I'm to be completely honest with ya, it's starting to freak me out."

Tom chuckled to himself as he raised his cup again. "Anyway, enough of that, how'd things go at the dentist?"

"Oh that, yes fine, thanks, I'd dislodged a filling, that's why I had to chase for an emergency cancellation, luckily I got one, anyway it's been sorted now. How's work, how's Carl? I haven't seen you out with him for ages."

"Oh, he's just fine, we've got a new case we're working on," Tom said, "still early days, not sure where it's going just yet."

Jess could see Tom eyeing an ashtray placed on the table between them. It had been pushed to one side by someone who had sat there previously. It had a couple of recently discarded butts in it.

"And the no smoking, how's that going for you?" Jess asked as if already knowing the answer, given his fixation on the ashtray, she felt he was only one small step away from salivating at the sight of the discarded butts.

"So far so good," Tom replied. "Don't look so shocked. This is gonna make you laugh, I've had a couple of sessions of hypnosis or hypnotherapy or whatever you wanna call it, but it seems to be working. Certainly, a damned sight better than gum or those patches, that's for sure."

Tom had undergone weekly sessions of hypnosis. It was only when he stated this as having taken place since he last saw Jess did he realise just how long it had been since they last enjoyed spending time together. Aside from the previous date that they had missed, given Tom's shifts they had found it tricky to get time off to coincide with each other.

"Hypnosis, wow, maybe I should give it a try about my vertigo," Jess laughed. "What made you go for that?"

"Can't remember who mentioned it exactly, glad they did though, the money I've paid for the sessions is far outweighed by what I've saved in fags."

"Well, you're certainly smelling better, you used to reek of it when you'd come around after work, no offence, hun," Jess said.

"Whilst we're on that subject, how about dinner at mine on Friday after work?" Tom asked.

Jess was always curious about Tom's work, she wanted to ask about his current investigation.

"I'd love to," she replied, "what time?"

"I dunno just yet, can I let you know when I know what time I'll be finishing work?" Tom replied.

The nature of police work meant that the time a shift ended did not guarantee that being when you'd actually finish work. If Tom was in the middle of something when his shift ended he may not be in the position to just drop it to pick up again on his next shift. As a result, there had to be a certain flexibility to any plans made beyond the end of a shift.

"Of course." Jess answered, "how come you're not sure where your current investigation is going just yet?"

"Well," — Tom paused to take another sip of his coffee, and to have a quick look round to make sure no one was in earshot — "we've got a victim, MO doesn't make sense, and no suspect details just yet."

The *MO* refers to *modus operandi* which is someone's habits of working, particularly in the context of criminal investigations. It is a Latin phrase, approximately translated as "method of operation". In English, it is often shortened to *MO*.

The term is often used in police work when discussing crime and addressing the methods employed by the perpetrators. It is also used in criminal profiling, where it can help in finding clues to the offender's psychology. It largely consists of examining the actions used by the individual(s) to execute the crime, prevent its detection and/or facilitate escape. A suspect's *modus operandi* can assist in their identification, apprehension, and can also be used to determine links between crimes.

"It's bizarre what we've got to work with. The victim's a gang member, total scrote, who's OD'd, but with no history of drug usage, and has been dumped in the middle of nowhere."

"I take it you've ruled out suicide then?" Jess replied. She knew she was stating the obvious, otherwise Tom wouldn't be investigating.

"Yeah, there's definitely someone yet to be accounted for, he's our main player. We've not got much to go on, just working our way through those who know him. With this sort of thing it's usually personal."

"Good luck with that, and say hi to Carl for me, we really should get him and Becky out again soon."

"Sounds good to me, I'll mention it to him when we're both back in the office," Tom replied. "Like I say, Friday will have to be on a phone call though, can't guarantee what time I'll get out of work if that's okay? What do you wanna do, restaurant or takeaway or are you volunteering to cook?"

"I'm happy to cook, I'll do slow-cooked lamb shanks, that way they'll be ready whenever you are, and I can just bring the whole thing over with me, how's that?"

"Perfect," Tom said.

They hadn't actually seen each other for a couple of weeks so neither of them was in a rush to tear themselves away.

Unfortunately, the time came when Jess had to go. This prompted them both to sort themselves out ready to leave.

Tom stood up and checked the contents of his pockets. After the events of the previous couple of weeks, he was now paranoid that he would misplace or lose something.

He took his keys from his jacket pocket and placed them on the table, so he could locate everything else before finding a place for them.

"I can't believe you still carry that!" Jess exclaimed at seeing Tom's keys on the table.

She was referring to a Lego key ring trinket she had bought for him after their first date.

It was a Lego policeman figure. More specifically the *Bad Cop* character from the Lego Movie of the same name that was released around the same time they started dating. The *Good Cop / Bad Cop* character which was voiced by Liam Neeson in the movie. It marked an early date for them, one they remembered fondly as they were the only ones there without children.

It may have been bought as a joke by Jess, but Tom was taken back when she handed it to him, and as a result it was the only trinket he had on his keys and it meant a great deal to him.

After Tom had assured himself that everything had a place he reclaimed his keys from the table. He held them in his open hand, he looked at them and specifically the little Lego man grimacing back at him in his mirror shades and motorcycle crash helmet.

Tom, smiled. "Why wouldn't I?" he questioned.

"I only bought it as a joke, never thought you'd actually keep it," Jess replied with a chuckle.

Tom took one last look at the figure. It had become battered in the time since he had been given it *as a joke*. He placed his keys back in his pocket.

"It goes with me wherever I go," he said. "Have you got everything?"

"Yep," Jess replied, "I'm ready."

"Let's go then," Tom said, "see you on Friday."

"Definitely," came the reply.

They kissed briefly before leaving in opposite directions.

Day 8

"Good days off?" Carl asked of his sergeant.

Carl had started work earlier than Tom. He was already at his desk reviewing another report when Tom came into the office.

"Yeah, not too bad mate. Didn't do a great deal, met Jess for a coffee the other day, but that's about it. She says *hi* by the way."

"How's things with you guys?"

"Oh, definitely better than they have been, be better still if I didn't keep forgetting things between us. She'll be adamant we've arranged something, then only reminds me *after* I've forgotten it. She's suggesting we all get together sometime."

"Yeah, we'll certainly be up for that, let me know when so we can get a sitter in."

Unlike Tom who was a forty-something bachelor, Carl was younger, in his late thirties, with a wife, Becky and two children – one at primary school and the other at pre-school.

"Will do," Tom replied, "have we got the tox report back yet?"

The tox report referred to the report from the coroner's office which contained the results of the blood analysis taken from Burgess' body during his autopsy.

"Yep, just been scanning through it" b — Carl indicated to the open report in front of him — "it's like we thought; massive heroin overdose, but no prior evidence of any IV drug usage. No track marks or anything else to suggest prior drug usage."

Track marks refer to historic puncture wounds from intravenous (IV) drug use. These are typically in the crook of the elbow, but sometimes the back of the knees or the feet are used.

"The only two puncture wounds found were in the left elbow. Half the amount of heroin in his bloodstream would've been enough to kill him, enough presumably in a single injection, let alone doubling the dose. Someone's making a point, I'd say."

"That is bizarre." He remembered back to the property forms. "Two puncture wounds yet only one needle recovered at the scene. Was it dropped by accident?" Tom paused. "Also, another user isn't likely to want to waste any gear, so what's his point? Anything else?"

"Not really, no external trauma to the body, nothing apparently inhaled or ingested, it is pretty much as we see it. And again, the intel report states no drug-related offences, like you say, bizarre."

Tom set his jacket on the back of his chair.

"Do you want a coffee?" he said to Carl. Carl raised an empty mug indicating a *yes*. Tom took the mug as he walked past Carl.

Carl's mug was obviously a gift from his children. It was painted in blue and yellow squares to emulate the *Battenberg* effect of police cars. It also had Carl's warrant number and surname on it. Tom's looked plain in comparison, he was unaware of its origin. Without asking he knew what the order would be; coffee, white with two sugars.

A couple of minutes later Tom returned and set the mug down on Carl's desk.

"Ta," said Carl, "don't bother getting comfy, I've just had a call from Eddie over in Chesterton CID, they've just had an untimely death that's currently deemed as suspicious. He's emailed me the report. I'm just going to print it off now."

Carl got up and went to the printer.

It was common practice for neighbouring forces to share intelligence on patterns of offending and known transient offenders. However, it was more of a courtesy to share details of individual cases. Eddie was a long-time friend of them both. He used to work with Carl before transferring to another force to make his journey to work easier.

As a result, they often shared details of the cases they were working on the off-chance it was of interest to the other. In this instance, an *untimely death* wouldn't necessarily be something to make it across to a neighbouring force at this early stage.

An untimely death is the term given to a deceased when it was unexpected. This can range from anything from a cancer-riddled octogenarian all the way to a fit and healthy twenty-something collapsing and dying on the football pitch. Until it has been ruled as non-suspicious, police are informed, and all the necessary procedures are put in place to secure and preserve evidence as well as documenting any chain of events.

Carl arrived back from the printer. Instead of simply putting the printed pages down on the desk whilst he put his coat on he put the report between his teeth.

"Ready when you is," he said.

The degree of urgency wasn't shared by Tom. He was still sitting at his desk. His mug of coffee was being held with both hands. He took one more sip before setting the mug down. He stood and took his jacket from the back of his chair. He looked down at his cup, though uninspired in its appearance it contained yet another coffee that would now go undrunk.

"Okay," he said, "let's go, you can drive."

oOo

Much like the routine of a few days earlier, Carl drove whilst Tom flicked through the details of the report that Eddie had emailed across.

It contained only very basic details. It gave the name and date of birth of the deceased as being Ronald Campbell, aged sixty-eight. The report stated that the police had been called after he had missed an appointment with his general practitioner. The surgery had become concerned and when they couldn't make contact with Campbell they called the police and asked them to attend his address to do a welfare check.

Then, when the officer attended Campbell's home address he saw the occupant in bed through a narrow gap in the curtains, and with no answer to repeated knocking the officer effected entry by breaking a window. It was then, based on this officer's observations, that the CID became involved.

The address was just over the border into the neighbouring force's area. In reality, it took less time to get there than it did to attend the scene of Burgess' untimely demise the previous week.

This wasn't Tom or Carl's investigation. They were invited to attend the location as a courtesy between forces in case of any links that may become apparent. This would cause delays in their own enquiries, but it was a necessary evil.

oOo

It wasn't long before they found the familiar sight of a police investigation. As Carl pulled into Campbell's road they saw a number of police vehicles parked ahead of them. Carl parked where he could, and they approached on foot.

Before they reached the boundary of the premises, Carl spotted Eddie on the pavement on his phone. He watched and waited for Eddie to finish his call before approaching him.

"Eddieeeeeeeee," Carl said as Temporary Detective Inspector Poulton walked up and shook his hand.

"How's it going, buddy?" Eddie asked.

"All good here, mate, how's thing's with you?"

"Ask me that again in a couple of hours will ya?" Eddie looked a little unsettled.

"I'll let you in on what I know. Morning, Tom," Eddie said as Tom approached.

Tom smiled and nodded. "Morning."

"Not a great deal to say at the moment," Eddie began.

As they were away from the premises Eddie took a silver tin from his pocket, roughly the size of a deck of playing cards. It was a cigarette rolling machine.

He opened the tin and took out a pack of cigarette papers, he took out a single paper and put it between his teeth as he started to talk.

"Well, as you know the guy in there is a Ronald Campbell, aged sixty-eight, lives alone, no immediate family that we're aware of."

Eddie took a pinch of tobacco from the tin and spread it evenly across the rolling mat of the machine.

"What you probably don't know about Mr Campbell is that he was on bail awaiting trial for a string of historic sexual offences against young boys."

Eddie then took the paper from between his teeth and laid it expertly along the length of the mat. He then put the machine to his face and licked the edge of the paper.

"Y'see, Mr Campbell who lives here used to be a scout leader who liked keeping the boys, shall we say, *company* on camps."

Eddie closed the lid of the tin and out popped a perfectly rolled cigarette. He cleaned up the ends and put it in his mouth.

He placed the tin back in his pocket and fumbled in there for his lighter.

After finding the lighter he lit the cigarette and took that first puff.

"How's the no smoking going, Tom, still fighting the good fight?" he said as if expecting Tom to ask for one himself.

"So far so good," Tom replied with a defiant smile. He was surprised that his little crusade had become news in the neighbouring force.

"Good for you," Eddie said. "Well, the reason we all find ourselves here on this beautiful morning is because plod pushed the alarm button."

Plod was a derogatory term sometimes used by plain-clothes officers to describe their uniformed counterparts.

"They attended after he missed an appointment with his GP, saw the deceased in bed, forced entry. No obvious signs of a struggle *but* they believe someone else may have been in the property as the bolts on the front door hadn't been thrown. It was just shut on the latch. Come on, I'll take you inside."

Eddie led the trio to the officer at the end of the driveway. They hadn't gone all out with the barrier tape as had been done at the Burgess scene because it was deemed that the perimeter of the premises formed a natural boundary, with a single officer keeping the log.

Eddie booked Tom and Carl into the log and they all went up the sloped drive to the front of Campbell's home.

Looking at the building addressed Tom's first curiosity. He wondered how the first officer on scene had seen the deceased through his bedroom window. This had now been addressed – it was a semi-detached bungalow.

First of all, Eddie led Tom and Carl around the back of the building. The back garden could be accessed without having to go through any gate.

He led them to the window nearest the adjoining wall with the neighbour.

They could see that the curtains hadn't been drawn, but there was enough of a gap to see through into the bedroom, and with the sun rising behind them it cast a brilliant beam of sunlight into the room.

This clearly showed a male figure of large stature lying in bed. The covers had now been completely discarded from the bed, but Tom visualised the scene how the first officer must have seen it.

Tom stepped back from the window and looked down towards his feet. The area immediately under the window was paved giving no opportunity for any forensics. Tom then surveyed the garden. It was surrounded by what was most likely a six-foot-high panelled fence with a trellis above it. The trellis appeared to be intact suggesting that this hadn't been scaled to gain access to the rear of the property.

Mind you, with the back garden insecure who would need to? Tom thought.

"Come on, guys, I'll take you inside," Eddie said.

Both the front door and the back door were rather unusually on the side of the property. Both were now open and in use. They had created an impromptu one-way system through the property.

This wasn't Tom or Carl's investigation. They weren't here to draw any conclusions or have any input. As a result, they wouldn't be speaking to neighbours or any other officers in attendance unless it was absolutely necessary.

Tom wanted to view the property and the scene for himself before discussing anything more with Carl or Eddie. This allowed him to come to an unbiased conclusion, rather than have it tainted with conjecture and speculation.

Tom entered the back door, the door furthest from the street, by himself. He had put on a pair of examination gloves as well as a pair of elasticated overshoes which, as before, were similar in appearance to a shower cap.

Once inside the kitchen, Tom acknowledged the others who were already there. He had placed his warrant card on its lanyard outside of his jacket, so everyone could see he had authority to be there. Tom knew from experience that it was easier to do it this way than to be challenged by those who didn't recognise him.

Tom then went into the hallway and then into the bedroom. The bedroom was currently in the process of being examined and photographed by the SoCO. Tom could see the deceased lying on his back in the middle of a double bed. He was wearing striped pyjama trousers and a whitish vest. It was once white but had become faded and stained over time.

Campbell appeared to be a very large man. Tom wasn't sure how much of this was his normal self and how much was as a result of post-mortem bloating. Following death, gases form within the body and these expand over time giving an impression of distention.

The bedroom itself was unremarkable. It didn't show anything of the personality of the person who slept in there. Apart from the bed, the room was sparsely furnished, with a single wardrobe, a dressing table and two bedside tables with shaded lamps on them.

As the curtains hadn't been drawn the room was relatively dark, and as a result was being illuminated by the ceiling light and supplemented by a battery-powered tripod lamp that the SoCO had brought in.

This low-level lighting of the tripod lamp highlighted something for Tom.

He approached the bedside table furthest from the window, closest to where he had entered the room.

He crouched down to scrutinise what he had seen in closer detail.

Apart from being filthy and absolutely caked in dust, this bedside table had only one thing on it, a shaded lamp. It was this that had Tom's attention. With the low-level lighting from the SoCo's tripod light, Tom could see that the lamp wasn't sitting in the ring of dust that had been previously made for it. He could see under the bulbous base of the lamp that would have been shadowed by the ceiling light, or indeed by the lamp itself. More so, there were marks made in the dust next to it.

The disturbance in the dust suggested that the lamp may have been knocked at some point and reset to where it was believed it had originally sat. *Was this as a result of a struggle, or had it just been bumped when a cup or glass had been set next to it?* he wondered.

Tom stood back up and surveyed the room.

"Excuse me," the SoCO said politely.

Tom realised he was now getting in the way and he didn't need to be there. They had work to do so he'd let them get on with it.

As Tom stepped back into the hallway he could see Carl and Eddie in the kitchen. Carl saw him and acknowledged him.

Tom then carried on along the hallway. He passed the bathroom on his right and then went into the living room.

This room looked like it belonged in another house. It was immaculate, *and* it was creepy.

Knowing what Tom now knew about Campbell made this room feel like the Child Snatcher's lollipop wagon out of *Chitty Chitty Bang Bang*.

Around the walls were photos from Campbell's days as a scout leader. In all of them he was surrounded by groups of young boys, and in all of them he was smiling broadly. A broad smile on a chubby bespectacled face. His hands couldn't be seen in any of the pictures. A look of disgust fell across Tom's face as he wondered where his hands actually were when the photos were taken.

Around the room on every available flat surface were toys covering all ages of interest. They were positioned on the sideboard, on the coffee table and in the corner on shelves. There were wooden pre-school building blocks. They weren't just sat in a pile, they were built into buildings and towers. Action figures were posed as if in battle with each other.

The toys weren't just biased towards the boys either. In the corner was a large armchair, and on it were rag dolls and plush bears and other furry animals.

In the far corner opposite the door was a free-standing corner shelving unit. From where Tom stood, he could see that on every shelf there were trinkets and toys of Disney characters and from other movies.

Everything in this room was a dust trap, but everything was pristine. This room must have been dusted on a daily basis to keep it as clean as it was today.

Carl entered the room behind him.

"Have you seen all this?" Tom said to him.

"Yeah, gave me the fucking creeps," Carl replied.

Tom had a last look around the room. Just as he turned back towards the door to exit the room something caught his eye.

On the top shelf of the free-standing corner unit, standing with almost pride of place on the shelf of pristine trinkets, toys and ornaments, he saw something that appeared to have absolutely no place in this room whatsoever.

On the shelf smiling back at him was a single Lego figure. That in itself didn't seem too odd, but this Lego figure was battered and scored as if through rough play. Also, it appeared to have once been a key ring as it had the metal hoop still attached to its head, but the chain and split-ring were now missing.

But most bizarrely and coincidentally it was the *Bad Cop* character from the *Lego Movie*, similar to that which Tom had on his keys, the one that Jess had bought for him as a joke and that they had laughed about only days earlier.

Tom reached into his jacket pockets to find his keys to look at his own one. His keys weren't there.

"Bollocks," he said to himself.

He knew it was nothing more than a coincidence about the key ring, but nevertheless, it bothered him for the remainder of the time he and Carl spent at Campbell's house and for the duration of the journey back. His bother consumed his attention and as a result he appeared distracted. However, he denied anything was wrong when Carl noticed and made enquiries.

oOo

Again, Tom tried not to show his haste when he got back to the police station.

"I'm busting for a piss, I'll see you upstairs," he said to Carl as he went to park the car.

It was any excuse to get back to his desk as quickly as he could.

When he was at his desk, he rapidly went through the drawers. He checked the top ones, then further down.

In his panic to find his keys, he missed what he was looking for. On the top of his desk, behind his now cold, half-drunk coffee in his uninspiring mug, were his keys.

Tom saw them. Grabbed them. He looked at them, there wasn't a Lego figure key ring anywhere in sight.

There was a split-ring with a couple of links of chain attached. But it had nothing attached to it.

"What the fuck?" he said to himself.

He sat down trying to get a grasp of the situation. It just didn't add up for him. Only a few days ago it was definitely there. It was obvious that Jess had seen it because she had made comment on it. But he had got so used to it being there that he didn't notice it himself from one day to the next.

Again, Tom searched all of the pockets of his jacket and all the drawers of his desk.

He sat down, resigned to the fact that it was gone, and at the very least wasn't here at work. If it had fallen off prior to today the chances are it would have been vacuumed up by the cleaners by now.

"Feel better?" Carl said as he approached the desks.

It was then he saw the look of confused frustration on Tom's face.

"What's up, did you lose something?" he said.

Tom couldn't wait for the day to finish. He was busy, but he was distracted. He had even gone out to his car during his meal break to search for the missing key ring, but nothing was to be found either in his car or on the walk to it.

It had nothing to do with the fact that it was a sentimental gift from his girlfriend that he had lost, it was the fact that something identical had ended up, completely out of place, on the shelf of a now-deceased suspected paedophile.

For someone who was trained and taught not to believe in coincidences, that's exactly what Tom was trying to put this down to.

oOo

That evening Tom turned his flat upside down looking for the key ring. He went through the waste bin and the vacuum cleaner bag with no success.

He was checking all the pockets of all his coats, jackets and trousers when his phone buzzed indicating a text message received.

"For fuck's sake," Tom said as he was getting increasingly frustrated.

He interrupted the search to view the message. It was from Carl.

It read: *They're going to be investigating it as a murder, there's evidence to suggest he may have been suffocated, see you tomorrow.*

That's just fucking great Tom thought. Not only was he having a difficult time convincing himself that this was nothing more than a coincidence, but now it was a coincidental murder.

DAY 10

Although the Burgess killing was his investigation and he had absolutely no responsibility for the Campbell case, Tom found himself distracted by what he was hoping was nothing more than a mere coincidence.

He still hadn't found his key ring. This bothered him. He had it a few days earlier when he met Jess for a coffee, yet when he needed to lay his hands on it, it was nowhere to be seen.

But this wasn't the only thing bothering him, Tom's investigation into the unexplained death of Liam Burgess had come up against a brick wall. The forensics report had drawn a blank, and there appeared to be nothing in the way of motive to link his death to any of his criminal associates.

All the coroner's report was able to conclude was that death was as a result of a massive heroin overdose. No other suspicious substances were found in or on the body. That in itself muddied the waters even further because Burgess had no previously reported incidents involving drug use or supply.

The only indication of another person interacting with the body was a number of shoe prints in the soil. Size eight shoe prints.

Tom himself wore a size eight. This, however, was more of a feasible coincidence. One that Carl had joked with him about when the SoCO measured the print and determined the sizing when they had attended the scene where Burgess' body was found.

Reminding himself about the missing key ring Tom felt compelled to again check the drawers of his desk and the area directly beneath them in the vague hope that the cleaners weren't that thorough in their efforts. But still it was nowhere to be found. Although he was determined to find his trinket, he drew the line at sending out an office-wide email to ask if any of his colleagues had found it, for fear of ridicule.

Similarly, Tom didn't want to call Eddie Poulton and ask him if he could revisit Campbell's home address. He had no reason to, and anything to the contrary would raise questions. Questions that Tom wouldn't have the answers for, answers that he didn't have, and even if he did he wouldn't be prepared to give.

Carl wasn't working today. He still had some time off owing. Despite the investigation being where it was Tom said he could take the day off.

Tom sat back in his chair and stared at his computer screen, it had been a few minutes since he used it, so it had defaulted back to the screen saver which was the force's crest bouncing around the screen. He sat with his hands behind his head with his fingers interlaced.

Thinking about the Campbell case reminded him of a murder investigation he had been a part of several years ago where the victim was also a publicised paedophile.

Campbell was a former scout leader who preyed on the boys in his charge. Tom's previous investigation had involved a man named Malcolm Finlay. He was believed to be a member of a national network of paedophiles involved in travelling the country to approach young girls and sometimes boys after initially posing as children their own age online until it was too late, and then traffic them around with the eventual goal of introducing them to others to engage in underage sex.

Finlay had been arrested and charged with the lesser offence of possessing indecent images after he had taken his laptop in for repair. It was believed his behaviour was far more decadent but was yet to be proven.

It was during this interim, as Finlay awaited his court date for the indecent images charge, that a group of cyber vigilantes responded to his continued online messages pretending to be a young girl seeking friendship. They replied with everything they knew he would want to read. They had even sent googled images in response to his sordid requests.

Then came the inevitable request and suggestion that they met. The day and time were agreed on Finlay's terms, following something of a protest and indecision on the part of the group's portrayal of the *girl* to allay any suspicion. Finlay had suggested the location, one which he knew fairly well, but it was an area that the *girl* claimed she didn't know. An area she would have to get trains and buses to reach.

Finlay had told the girl where he would be parked and the make, model and colour of his car. He claimed to only be a couple of years older than the girl, making the ownership of a car feasible.

He had arrived in good time, ready and waiting for his next target to arrive. She never turned up. But Finlay wasn't going to be spending his evening alone.

What he realised, all too late, was that he had been set up. It was only then that the remoteness of the location he had chosen was to ultimately go against him.

Finlay's car was found with the windows smashed. Finley himself was found nearby. He didn't have a scratch on him.

He was found hanging upside down from a tree. His hands bound behind his back and duct tape across his mouth.

He could have survived the duration of his ordeal, between being strung up and when he was finally discovered, had it not been for the fact that he was undergoing treatment for pneumonia. As a result of the condition Finlay essentially drowned in his own mucus.

Despite scrutiny of all of Finlay's computers and mobile phones, no one was identified as being responsible for setting up the ambush which ultimately led to his death, and there were no forensics at the scene. As a result, the case was closed pending any new information.

That was deemed to be a fitting and symbolic demise for a paedophile, although the grizzly details of the incident were kept from the media to prevent any such vigilante group relishing the publicity and highlighting their cause.

What puzzled Tom was why a person such as Campbell, similar in many ways to Finlay, was then killed in his own bed. The perceived purpose of such an incident was not only to punish those involved but also to send a message out to like-minded individuals, hence the details of Finlay's death were never made public. What had happened to Campbell was unlikely to make any headlines beyond his obituary.

Tom was curious to know Campbell's cause of death. Out of curiosity, he typed out an email to Eddie asking for that information when he had it.

That wasn't the only revelation. Tom was also curious about the commonalities between the two investigations.

So far only one commonality existed –

Him.

Tom had also previously investigated the murder of a gang member such as Burgess.

Two murders, in essence independent of each other with absolutely nothing to link them, happening within a week of each other, and local, albeit in the jurisdiction of neighbouring police forces. There was certainly nothing to link one to the other, except Tom's increasing curiosity. One he was assigned to investigate, the other he couldn't ignore that something personal to him linked him to the scene.

With the time Tom had left of this shift he decided to scour the current and recently historic unexplained deaths, as well as any murders under investigation. The reason for his curiosity was to see if there had been any recent incidents that had a similar modus operandi, or *MO* to any case that he had previously been involved with.

He started his search in an ever-increasing radius. This, to his surprise, revealed a significant number of results. Tom was quite shocked to see just how many unexplained deaths there had been within his force and the surrounding areas in the last few months. Not all of these were, or be reclassified as, a murder or unlawful killing. A lot would be considered as an untimely death, natural causes, a suicide or left as unexplained. There were too many to scrutinise each individual report in any great detail.

However, he then cross-referenced the same parameters but this time including dates. In the first instance, Tom included only the reports within the last month.

This showed a search result of eight reports. Tom was able to instantly discount the majority based on the age of the deceased, as he had never been involved in a case when the victim had been over seventy years of age.

That left two reports that would need to be looked at in greater detail. Tom noted down the report reference numbers. He opened the first report which was the first one to occur in chronological order.

This report centred around a stabbing.

Tom started to read from the report. The MO on the front page showed a one paragraph overview of what was perceived to be the actions of those involved. Tom read it in a mumbled voice,

"During hours of darkness in an alleyway between two semi-detached dwellings in a quiet residential street has approached the victim and stabbed him before removing items from pockets leaving the empty wallet and keys nearby." Tom paused realising this was as far as he needed to read.

"A street robbery gone wrong," he concluded as he exited the report. This report did not contain any of the similarities that Tom was looking for.

He opened the last report that had met the search criteria.

Once again Tom scanned the front screen down to the MO. Again, Tom read it in the same mumbled voice.

He preferred to read crucial elements aloud as it was then received by two senses, hearing and sight, as opposed to just one. This way it gave him greater clarity and understanding as well as slowing the process and prevented him from inadvertently scan-reading the document.

"Early evening on upper floor of a retail park car park, approached victim as she was sat in her driver's seat and caused a single puncture wound to the back of her neck."

Again, Tom paused, but for reasons different to before.

"Car park, single puncture wound."

Tom looked at the notes he had taken showing the report reference numbers. He crossed out the first, and ringed the second, stabbing the page with a full-stop before setting his pen down.

Tom started to go behind the front screen into the report itself. He wanted to know more about the victim, the location that the incident took place as well as an overview of the investigation.

"Victim, female, thirty-seven years of age. Location, floor three, Five Oaks Shopping Centre car park."

Tom made notes of the bullet points as they were occurring to him.

The victim's vehicle was a five-door Audi A1. No child seats. Tom read that the vehicle was immaculate, no indication that the owner was a family person. There was nothing to suggest that children ever travelled in the car.

The SoCO report stated that the car had been thoroughly examined inside and out. But not a single identifiable print or trace evidence was found.

Although the interior was immaculate, the car's exterior was in need of a wash. As a result, one thing had been concluded from the examination.

The killer entered the car through the nearside rear door. The one furthest away from the driver's seat. This was deduced by the smudging to the dirt that had collected on the handles as well as smudges on the lower half of the doorframe suggesting that someone, possibly the killer, had crouched and leant against the door. The only other door with similar smudges was the driver's door itself.

Tom looked at a couple of still images that had been taken from the CCTV within the car park that had been attached to the report.

The footage showed the victim walking away from her car and locking it. This was seen in a short sequence of images that showed the indicator lights flashing suggesting that the central locking had been activated.

Tom then looked at the victim profile. Pauline Barnes was a domiciliary carer for the elderly. She was single, never married. She had no prior reason to contact the police, also no reason to suggest she was specifically targeted, and no indication there was anyone with a grievance against her with the inclination to go to this extreme.

Tom scanned ahead. There was no explanation to suggest when the killer entered the car. It was, however, suggested by the officer in charge of the investigation that the killer entered the car as the victim was loading her shopping into the boot.

Although this was a plausible time to enter the vehicle Tom didn't agree and shook his head as he read it.

Tom recalled a clip from social media that went out across America as a warning to people to check their car after locking it and before leaving it.

It involved someone crouching down on the side away from the driver as they alighted from the vehicle. That someone would then open an opposite door to the driver's door, the nearside rear door just a crack. The owner would then habitually walk off and press their remote to lock the car. They may possibly look back to see the indicators blink and walk away thinking all was in order.

What they were unaware of is that when one door is open none will lock although the indicators may still blink in the attempt to lock the vehicle.

Tom felt that this would explain the smudges to the nearside rear door.

The car had a ticket placed on the dashboard indicating that the victim only intended to be away from the car for up to the thirty minutes of free parking that the car park offered.

Knowing this, the killer could lay in wait within the car, or return short of the expiration time pending the victim's return, or even follow her around the shops and then beat her back to the car. Tom's hunch would be that the killer would probably lay in wait in the back seat for the victim to return, put her bags in the boot and then finally, to sit back in the driver's seat. Otherwise, if the killer left the car themselves they would risk having to rush back and draw unnecessary attention to themselves.

Tom again looked at the CCTV images. The victim returned to her car less than twenty-three minutes after leaving it. The same cars were parked either side of her vehicle as could be seen in the images.

The investigation report stated that the footage from which the still images were obtained did not show any person on foot approach the victim's vehicle apart from the victim herself.

Tom could see from the images that there was a possibility that someone could approach her car by walking along the wall that the parked cars were facing. If they were to keep low enough they would be completely obscured from the CCTV by the parked vehicles. So, if none of the vehicles had moved in the time the victim was away then it was a safe bet to assume that the killer could have left in that fashion too.

Tom found it difficult to believe that there was nothing internally in the vehicle to suggest that someone had been laying across the back seat.

The SoCO report stated that the victim's keys were found in the ignition, and that she had her seatbelt on. Tom clicked on the hyperlinks to view images showing both.

Tom started to read the report from the coroner's office. This stated that the cause of death was by a single puncture wound to the cerebellum. The autopsy revealed that the device used to make the wound was pointed as opposed to having a blade and was approximately 150 millimetres, or six inches long. Again, there were hyperlinks to show the described detail from the report.

Tom viewed the autopsy photos. The victim looked young, certainly younger than her age suggested. She was of slight build. There certainly didn't appear to be any fight in her. There were no signs of trauma to the body aside from the wound to the neck.

Except, as Tom progressed through the report it was stated that there was superficial trauma to the back of the scalp. Tom reviewed the earlier images. The victim also had a ponytail.

"She leaves the car, killer opens rear door, she's convinced she's left her car locked. Returns after twenty plus minutes. Puts her bags in the boot. Gets in the car, buckles up, keys in the ignition." Tom paused to catch up with his thoughts.

"The killer is lying in wait in the backseat watching, as she bends forward to put keys in the ignition the killer sits up and grabs her by her ponytail before shanking her in the back of the neck. Single wound. Then leaves."

Tom then scrolled through a few more pages of reports. Aside from the photographic images of the victim, her car, and the location, was a close-up of a button from an item of clothing. Tom scanned the report to determine its relevance.

"Ah, here it is," he muttered to himself, "a single button found discarded within close proximity of the nearside rear door of the victim's vehicle."

He scrolled back to the descriptive details of the victim.

"A single woman, no previous police contact, no known grievances with anyone, and apparently nothing to connect victim to killer. Seemingly random, unless the killing itself has any significance, and all they've got to go on is a fucking button."

Tom made some more notes of the who, where and how before closing the report.

He looked at the clock on the wall. The time it showed didn't make sense to him. He checked his watch. His eyes opened in disbelief. He had gone into overtime looking at these reports.

Tom took off his glasses and rubbed his eyes. He checked his watch once more.

Realising that it was showing the correct time, he exited out of the reports. Just before he shut the computer down, Tom thought it best he checked his emails one last time. His inbox had probably a dozen new emails. Looking down the list, Tom realised that they could wait until he was back in the office. All except one, from Eddie.

Tom opened the message to find that, apart from the subject which had the name Campbell in it, the email itself contained only one word.

Smothered!!

Tom sucked his teeth as he factored the new information into the equation he was forming.

After closing the email and shutting down his computer, Tom stood up and backed away from his desk. He took his coat from the back of his chair. He was about to walk away from his desk. He stopped, realising he had forgotten something.

Tom looked at his desk and put his glasses, which were lying in front of his keyboard, back in their case. He began to turn away again, but again stopped. Tom tore the top sheet of paper from the pad, the sheet with the notes he'd just made on. He stuffed the unfolded sheet into his trouser pocket before leaving his desk. He thought it best to not leave such notes on display for anyone to see and scrutinise and draw their own conclusions.

Tom said, "Goodnight" to a couple of officers sitting at different desks on his way to the door. No responses came.

oOo

That evening after dinner Tom had given himself a chance to settle for the evening. As he prepared his clothes for his next shift by chance he happened to put his hand in the pocket of his trousers.

He took out the contents of the pocket; amongst some small change was a crumpled piece of notepaper. Tom instantly recalled what this was. He placed it on the counter surface in his kitchen and gave his best effort to flatten it out. His mind began racing.

Tom then snatched out a hand and took out a pen from a pot on the side, before searching frantically for a piece of paper. He conceded the search, instead resorting to using the back of the envelope of an unopened letter. He then scribbled some column headings as if preparing a spreadsheet.

Victim   Suspect   Location   MO

Tom then began to fill in some of the gaps under these headings utilising elements from these recent incidents:

Victim	Suspect	Location	MO
Gang Member (20s)		Woods	Drug O/d
Single Woman (30s)		Car Parks	Puncture Wound to head
Paedo (60s)		Home	Smothered

There were a lot of gaps on his chart, but there were some startling similarities. Not to each other, but with cases Tom had previously been involved with. Tom began recalling the details of the cases he had worked involving the elements that already had links, he then produced a second list including how the suspect was linked to the crime, as well as the outcome to the case:

Victim	Suspect	Location	Mo	Link	Result
Paedo (60s)	Lynch Mob	Wasteland	Strung Up	None	Unsolved
Gang Member (20s)	Rival Gang	Car Park	Punching Wound	DNA	Convicted
Woman (30s)	Husband	Home	Smothered	Confession	Suspect Suicide
Prostitute (18)	N/k	Woods	Drug O/d	Forensics	Unsolved

Tom then started to underline the commonalities between these two lists:

Victim	Suspect	Location	Mo	Link	Result
Paedo (60s)	Lynch Mob	Wasteland	Strung Up	None	Unsolved
Gang Member (20s)	Rival Gang	Car Park	Punching Wound	DNA	Convicted
Woman (30s)	Husband	Home	Smothered	Confession	Suspect Suicide
Prostitute (18)	N/k	Woods	Drug O/d	Forensics	Unsolved

This was starting to concern Tom. Three of the four most recent unexplained deaths matched various elements of cases he had previously worked. Not just the odd one or two elements though, but so far nine of the twelve main elements involving: who, where and how.

As a result, after he went to bed he had a very unsettled night.

DAY 12

Tom pondered his revelation for a couple of days. Although the commonalities between the current investigations and his previous case history were tenuous at best, Tom felt he had better err on the side of caution. Whether he'd be laughed at or listened to he felt it better to bring his observations and concerns to his line manager.

Tom's line manager was a Detective Inspector named Gordon Kilpatrick. He hadn't been Tom's supervisor for very long, he was only in the role on a temporary basis. But, the two had worked together on several cases over the years.

Tom felt comfortable with airing his concerns to Kilpatrick without fear of ridicule.

He had also considered speaking to Carl about this in the first instance. Although he hoped Carl would be forthright, Tom felt he would err on the side of caution and just tell him to "Go and see Kilpatrick".

Tom didn't want to just enter the DI's office to voice his concerns. His intention was to tag them onto the back of a review of the overall investigation in Burgess' death.

"I thought you'd quit smoking, Tom," Kilpatrick teased as Tom came into his office, shutting the door behind him.

"I have – I haven't had a fag in weeks," Tom replied. If he were being honest, he was getting sick of these continued jibes.

Tom had quit smoking weeks ago, and he hadn't touched a cigarette, or even felt the need for a vaporiser or gum since he'd started the hypnosis sessions.

"Yeah, yeah whatever. What is it then, maid on holiday since you quit?"

A puzzled look came across Tom's face.

Kilpatrick felt he had to explain his joke. "Your maid is away, no laundry getting done, your clothes still reek of old smoke, is it?"

Accepting defeat, Kilpatrick threw his hands up in the air and shook his head.

Tom obviously had other things on his mind.

Returning to decorum, Kilpatrick sat up straight and beckoned Tom to sit down.

"What can I do for you, Tom?"

"Well, sir, I just wanted to give you an overview of where we are with the Burgess case," Tom replied.

"And where are we, Tom?"

"We are coming up against a few dead ends at the mo. Tox report shows a massive heroin overdose, yet Burgess is by all accounts clean. He's OCG but *not* a user himself or even concerned in the supply, his next of kin haven't been able to give any positive lines of enquiry either." Tom paused for a moment to collect his thoughts.

"No known grievances against him which could've highlighted a suspect. Forensics has also drawn a blank. The only trace at the scene is a size eight shoe print, Carl's looking to finger me for it." Tom at last cracked a smile.

"Any leads at all?" Kilpatrick asked.

"We've gone out to all OCG's on the payroll, asking if they know anything, or why someone might target Burgess, but so far nothing. Either they don't know, or they know and are not saying for whatever reason."

Sometimes, those on the wrong side of the law can be persuaded to share information in exchange for financial reward, it's not a regular income, so they're not actually on the police payroll. They are known as a *CHIS*, a Covert Human Intelligence Source, which is defined as a person who establishes or maintains a personal or other relationship with another person for the covert purpose to disclose information. They are usually managed by a *handler* within the police.

"Okay, keep me updated on that will ya?" Kilpatrick asked. "Anything else?"

"Yes, sir." Tom paused, he was still contemplating discussing his sole reason for the actual meeting with the DI. He took a deep breath.

"I think someone may be trying to set me up."

Time appeared to stand still in Kilpatrick's office. A pin could've been heard to drop. Beyond the glass partitions life continued, for everyone but Tom and Kilpatrick.

"What makes you say that, Tom?" came the eventual and hesitant reply.

"Sir, locally we've had three unexplained deaths in the last couple of weeks, two here and one over in Wyevale. There are aspects linking me to all of them."

Tom stood up. He thought better on his feet. He started pacing the DI's office.

"I joked about the size eight's, but that's all that's linked me to the Burgess scene, so far anyway, but bear with me,"

Tom paused. He took another deep breath.

"Do you remember Jess?" Tom paused long enough to see Kilpatrick nod. "Well, she bought me a keepsake when we started seeing each other, it's a little Lego key ring of a motorbike cop, it's been on my keys for ages. Then the other day Carl and me go over to see Eddie Poulton in Wyevale to view his unexplained death. This job has since come back as a murder because a sixty-something sex offender was found smothered in his own bed."

Wanting to get things moving forward quicker than Tom was allowing, Kilpatrick interjected, "And how are you linked to this one?"

"The key ring was on a shelf in his front room," Tom replied vehemently.

"C'mon, Tom, are you sure it's one and the same?" Kilpatrick added trying to make sense of this situation.

"No, I'm not, but since seeing it there I've not been able to find mine anywhere. And I definitely had it only days before."

"Tom, this is just a coincidence, be realistic here. A size eight shoe print, for fuck's sake I expect half the office wear an eight. And a key ring? Coincidence, nothing more!"

"That's not all, Guv, I did some digging and found another job on our patch, I've not been involved in it in any way as I was tucked up on something else before being given Burgess' case. It's a stabbing, in a car park."

Tom looked at his DI, Kilpatrick's reaction suggested he was recalling the details of this investigation.

"No leads, nothing to go on. CCTV shows nothing. All they've got is a fucking button that was found on the ground near to the victim's vehicle."

"A button?" Kilpatrick queried.

"Yep, a single button was found beside her car."

"Wait, wait, wait," Kilpatrick interrupted, "*beside* the car? Beside the car is circumstantial at best. It's not evidence of any involvement, just *possibly* places its owner at the scene, it could've been kicked there."

"That's right, it is circumstantial, and as a single piece of evidence, it essentially proves nothing. But after reviewing that report I went home and looked at my jackets. One of them *does* have matching buttons."

"And? Is one missing Tom?" Kilpatrick was becoming impatient.

"Yes *and* no, it's not missing one from the cuffs or the front, but there isn't the spare that gets sewn into the lining."

"Maybe it never fucking had one, Tom, c'mon, *really*? I think you're making more of this than actually exists, I really do."

Tom put his hand into his trouser pocket and felt a folded piece of paper there.

He considered for a moment showing Kilpatrick his comparison list that showed the elements of recent incidents against historic investigations that he had drawn up.

He was in the process of taking it from his pocket when he thought better of it.

Seeing the confusion and distress in Tom's face, Kilpatrick felt he needed to again break the silence.

"Tom, take the rest of the day off, take a couple of days off if you need to, okay. You've said it yourself that the Burgess case has come up against a brick wall, so things aren't gonna fall behind," Kilpatrick said. "And do what you can to forget all this. I mean it, honestly, I feel it's nothing, really I do. But, I'll tell you what, I'll make a call over to Wyevale and ask for their report on their job, so I can review it myself, okay?"

Tom resigned himself to the situation. He nodded in agreement to his DI. Tom then headed back towards the door, he reached out and took hold of the handle, and turned his head to face back towards Kilpatrick. "Thanks, Guv," he said as he turned the handle and pulled open the door. Tom didn't wait for a reply as he exited the office.

Tom then went back to his desk. He found Carl sat across from him, he was leaning forward with his head propped up on one hand. Carl saw his DS return and sat up and turned to face him.

"Everything all right, boss?" Carl asked.

"Yeah, I'm gonna work from home for the rest of the day, okay, you can get me on my mobile if I'm needed."

There wasn't anything unusual about this so Carl didn't express any concern or feel the need to enquire any further.

oOo

What was unusual, however, was for Tom to be out of work during the working week. He felt at a loose end when he got back to his car.

His mind was elsewhere, so Tom walked past his car and continued into town.

Once there, he sat with a coffee outside of a coffee shop. The same coffee shop, and same table where he sat with Jess a week earlier. He reminisced about that occasion, and everything that had happened since then. Some things he could recall, but he realised he had blanks in his recollection, both before and since meeting Jess.

It was then he started to factor in other revelations, the DI Kilpatrick's dig about his quitting smoking, and Carl claiming he had seen him in town the other day. This just confused Tom and started to cause him frustration when he couldn't quantify it.

Tom then reverted back to his chat with the DI.

Am I just being ridiculous? Is this all nothing more than a coincidence? he thought.

He weighed up everything. His inspector was right, his jacket may very well never have had a spare button, and in any case, it would only ever be circumstantial evidence as they had agreed. It was certainly not enough to implicate anyone.

There was no evidence in hand to suggest that it was in fact his key ring on the shelf in Campbell's home. It *was* the only beaten up object in sight, and it was only *after* seeing it did he then realise *his* was missing, having consciously seen it only days before sat at that very table with Jess.

Then there was the shoe print, and his inspector was probably right, half of the staff in the office may very well wear a size eight.

Tom shook his head and smiled as he took a sip of his coffee. It was nearly cold. It was only then did he realise just how long he had sat there.

oOo

Later at home, Tom hung his coat up in the hallway cupboard. He felt compelled to again examine the coat from which the button could have come. Tom wasn't sure if it would be a perfect match, he was relying on memory to compare size and colour. They certainly looked similar with a marbled pattern to it, and his jacket was definitely missing a spare. Tom examined the internal seams and they appeared to be intact with no loose threads to suggest one had once been attached and since removed.

He had resigned himself to the fact that he was at the beginning of an enforced period of time off work. He wasn't on suspension, just told to take a couple of days off. With that he went into the routine he followed at the end of the working week.

He emptied his pockets: pieces of paper, keys, a pen and pocket debris were all placed on the kitchen counter. He then pulled the belt from his trousers before stripping them off and putting them in the washing machine. The same was done with the shirt he was wearing. He held it to his face and sniffed, maybe they had a point, the shirt wasn't as fresh as he would have believed.

For a moment, Tom was standing in his kitchen wearing only a pair of boxers. Having loaded the washing machine, he then went to his bedroom and slipped on t-shirt and jogging trousers.

Maybe I am just being ridiculous, he thought, and tried to think nothing more about it.

DAY 14

Because Tom didn't need to set an alarm, he woke when his body had finished sleeping as opposed to when his alarm dictated.

He lay in his bed, undecided whether to get up or stay there a while longer.

For reasons unknown to him, he had a thumping headache. The back of his head hurt. He rubbed it, he could feel an area of swelling. He looked at his hands. There was dirt on his fingers, no blood though from any injury to his head.

This puzzled Tom, but he thought nothing more of it as the time he had to contemplate it was short-lived. It was rudely interrupted by an increasingly loud knocking on his front door.

This immediately had reason to concern Tom because the communal areas of his block of flats were secure. No one was able to access the halls without a coded key fob or by a resident granting access via the entry-com system.

The entry-com control pad didn't have a *tradesman* button, which if installed allowed the postman and servicemen to enter the communal areas during daytime hours without having to seek permission.

In this instance, Tom thought it was either a neighbour or someone unknown.

The knocking became more persistent.

Tom was wide awake now, out of bed and dressing himself in the first clothes to hand, which were the t-shirt and joggers he had thrown down to the floor before he climbed into bed the previous evening.

Once dressed Tom went out into the hallway. He took a peek through the spy hole. He could see two men dressed in suits and a uniformed police officer.

"What the fuck!" Tom muttered under his breath.

Tom didn't have a clue what this might be about. He didn't recognise any of the people at his door. He certainly didn't work with any of them. *Why are they here?* he thought.

There was only one way to find out. Tom went to take off the security chain only to find it hadn't been used, it hung uselessly down the door frame. Tom had a well-versed routine of checking doors and windows before settling down, as well as whenever he left home. One trait that Tom had, along with many other police officers, was paranoia – expecting the worst and preparing for it. The fact that he had apparently gone to bed without securing the front door bothered him. He was adamant that he had, but routine leads to an unfamiliar familiarity, he could've forgotten doing it the previous evening with his recollection having been from the night before, or before that.

Brought back to the moment by yet another increasingly impatient knock, he unlocked the door, opened it fully and stood in the open doorway. He didn't say a word. He waited for one of those responsible for the rude awakening to break the silence.

"Tom Draven?" the suited man nearest him asked.

Tom nodded his reply as he rubbed sleep from his eyes.

The suited man reached into the inside pocket of his suit jacket and took out a small black folding wallet. He opened it with both hands and held it close to his body as he showed its contents to Tom.

"Tom, I am Inspector Peter Reynolds, Wyevale Police Station," he said in such a way as if he felt he shouldn't need such an introduction.

Tom simply stood there in silence and shrugged slightly as if indicating that Reynolds should continue.

"Tom, may we come in?" Reynolds asked.

"What's this all about?" Tom replied.

Reynolds accepted the fact that he wasn't going to be getting through Tom's front door without offering some more information.

"Okay, Tom, there's been an attempted murder, and we feel it might be linked to the Burgess case that you've been investigating. Can we come in so we can update you?"

"I'm on leave for a couple of days," Tom replied, "can't it wait until I'm back in the office, or better still talk to Carl, my DS, he'll be happy to help you guys out."

"I'm afraid I can't do that Tom, this involves *you*," Reynolds replied. His tone was becoming ever more solemn.

Tom looked across the faces of the three men standing in front of him. The other suited man and the uniformed PC had their gaze to the floor. It appeared that no one wanted to be there.

"I guess you'd better come in then," Tom said, eventually relenting.

Tom held the door open, allowing the three men to enter his flat. He gestured down the hallway which led towards his living room. As the last man passed him he closed the door and followed on behind the uniformed PC.

When they were all in Tom's living room he took a seat and gestured to them all to do the same.

Reynolds was the only one to take up Tom's offer.

The fact that the other two remained standing unnerved Tom somewhat, this did not feel in any way like a casual or friendly visit.

"Tom, I'm gonna get right to the point, I understand that you're an excellent and well-respected detective, so I'm not gonna bullshit you at all," Reynolds began.

Now Tom was started to feel nauseous. Suddenly the pain he felt in his head had left him as his mind had a new focus.

For some reason, he sensed what was about to come. He had been involved in everyone else's role in the room at one time or another.

Tom looked at the faces of the other two. They appeared to be looking at anything of interest around his living room to avoid making any eye contact with him.

"Tom, there was an attack last night, a young girl, prostitute, she was subdued and taken to some wasteland and her attacker tried to strangle her."

Reynolds paused as if he was looking, waiting for any noticeable reaction from Tom. "She fought him off and managed to escape, she made her way to the road where she was picked up and taken to hospital."

Reynolds paused again, he looked intently at Tom, trying to determine if any of what he had just said was provoking anything of a reaction from Tom. But instead, he looked bewildered.

"When she was interviewed at the hospital she gave a description of her attacker, her clothing was seized, swabs were taken, y'know the drill. We rushed the results of the swabs. Tom, they came back with your DNA."

A look of utter shock came over Tom's face. He again looked around the room, this time all eyes were on him. He couldn't believe what he had just heard. He was repeating to himself what had just been said to him, so much so he missed what happened next.

Reynolds had indicated towards the uniformed PC who had now stepped forward and began to address Tom. He was reading from a folded piece of paper that was resting on top of his open pocket notebook.

"Tom Draven, acting on information I have received I am arresting you on suspicion of the attempted murder of Leanne Young on the eighth of February. I am also arresting you on suspicion of the murders of Ronald Campbell in Chesterton on February second and Pauline Barnes in Five Oaks on the seventeenth of January." The officer paused to catch his breath. He then proceeded to caution Tom. Tom knew this part verbatim so he tuned out as the gravity of the situation was beginning to dawn on him.

"Tom, are you happy to leave dressed as you are?" Reynolds asked.

Tom's mind wasn't really in the moment. He was asked a question that needed a response, his immediate reaction was to just nod without having any understanding of what was being asked of him.

"All right then, let's get you out of here."

Tom rose to his feet, unsteady at first before finding his balance. He then started to walk towards the door back into the hallway. It felt like his feet weren't touching the ground. The uniformed PC took hold of his arm. Was this the escort technique taught in officer safety training, or was it the officer's kind efforts to steady him, to prevent him from collapsing? Either way, under these circumstances Tom was grateful for the assistance.

The PC then led Tom back along his hallway where he slipped on a pair of trainers that were by his front door, before leading him out of the flat and onto the communal landing. From there they both made slow progress downstairs as Tom held a firm grip of the bannister with his free hand before heading outside to a waiting police van.

As Tom was being loaded into the van he could see a police search team being briefed across the car park, as well as forensics officers readying their equipment.

There was a driver already in the van. The PC then sat alongside him in the front seats. The van slowly pulled away.

oOo

After being booked in to a custody centre that he had never visited before, Tom spent what seemed like hours sitting on a concrete slab that was meant to be a bed, and a wafer-thin laminated mattress which had probably sustained many a urine marinade.

During this time, he had only been taken from his cell to a medical room where an officer who he had never met before took hand swabs from him. This involved using a swab, similar in appearance to a cotton bud to rub the front and back of each hand. This is designed to collect any trace evidence to prove contact between persons involved.

Eventually, a rattling of keys was heard, and the heavy steel door was pulled open.

"Your brief's here, and some guy from the Fed," the Detention officer said.

The *guy from the Fed* referred to a representative of the Police Federation which is in essence the police's union. They would've appointed legal representation themselves and would want to be on hand to ensure Tom's needs were met.

Tom was led from his cell to a consultation room. The room was spacious, it had a bolted-down table and two benches as the only furniture. The table and benches were bolted to the floor, so they couldn't be used as a weapon. There was a yellow telephone affixed to the wall above the table to allow for private calls, and next to it was an alarm button for anyone who should need emergency assistance whilst in consultation with a prisoner.

Already in there were two men. One was dressed in a suit, he was sitting on one of the benches. The other was dressed more casually and was standing up but leaning against the back wall.

On seeing Tom enter, the seated one stopped scribbling notes, and the other stepped away from the wall.

"Hello, Tom, please have a seat," the seated man in a suit said.

Tom took a seat on the bench opposite him.

"Tom, I am James Reid of *Reid, Salmon & Hounslow Solicitors.* I have been appointed by the Police Federation."

The other man stepped up and introduced himself, "Hello Tom, I'm Kevin Buckhurst, I'm your Fed rep."

For almost an hour Tom answered the questions his legal team had for him. He was asked many questions about the offences to which he had been arrested, for which he couldn't give an explanation. For these questions, Tom simply stated he knew nothing.

"I wouldn't worry too much about that," Reid said.

Tom was then asked to confirm his whereabouts on the days in question. This he attempted but struggled to provide an account.

"That's more concerning," Reid replied. "Are you sure there's no one who could corroborate your whereabouts?"

Tom shook his head. "I don't think so."

"The custody record makes reference to you being forensically linked to the offences, are you able to elaborate on that for me?"

There was a long pause as Tom contemplated his next response. He thought back to the conversation he'd had with DI Kilpatrick.

Tom began to recount that conversation to Reid and Buckhurst. He explained the circumstantial links to the crime scenes of Barnes and Burgess and the absent key ring possibly linking him to Campbell. But whenever the questions came back to that of Leanne Young Tom was at a loss.

"Do you know of anyone who might want to stitch you up, either in the job or someone you've banged up?" Buckhurst added.

Tom shook his head. "Definitely no one in the job. Others? The list is endless."

Tom was referring to the countless suspects he'd investigated and had charged over the years who had received varying sentences.

"I think we're done here," Reid said. "Are you ready?"

"As I'll ever be," Tom replied.

oOo

A short while later, Tom was taken to an interview room. It was similar to the consultation room in size, décor and furnishing. Again, with a bolted-down table and benches. The only noticeable difference was the addition of an audio/visual recording device.

Tom and Reid had been led in by two of the men who were present when he was arrested. Detective Chief Inspector Peter Reynolds had already introduced himself. Tom now knew the other to be Detective Sergeant Lee Robertson. The only absence was the PC who had rendered kind assistance as he was taken from his flat.

During the formalities at the beginning of the interview, Tom had been asked to confirm his name and date of birth for the benefit of the recording. Once they had been completed Robertson began by reiterating the reason for Tom's arrest.

"You were arrested today on suspicion of the murder of Pauline Barnes in Five Oaks on the seventeenth of January, suspicion of the murder of Ronald Campbell in Chesterton on February the second, and the attempted murder of Leanne Young on the eighth of February. Please can you tell me what you know about these offences?"

"I can't," Tom replied.

"Can't?" Robertson replied, "can't or won't?"

"Can't," Tom emphasised. "I'm sure you've spoken to my DI, and I'm sure he's told you everything I've told him. I can't add anything to that."

"Okay, Tom, what were you doing on the seventeenth of January?"

"I'm sorry," Tom replied, "I don't recall."

Robertson repeated the questions for the second and eighth of February and appeared to be becoming increasingly frustrated by Tom's responses, or lack of.

Robertson had exhausted the open questions used to gain a comprehensive response. He then went onto closed questions, those requiring more a yes or no response.

With all the questions asked, Robertson then paused to flick through a few pages of the reports in front of him.

Eventually, he spoke again. "As was mentioned when you were arrested it was stated that you were forensically linked to the crime scenes of Young, Barnes and Campbell. Before I go on is there anything you want to say?"

Tom shook his head. He was understandably concerned, as so far everything else was circumstantial, in court forensic evidence is incontrovertible.

"Tom, after you were arrested today we conducted a search of your flat. We seized several items. One of which is a jacket that has a missing button. An identical button was found at the scene of the murder of Pauline Barnes."

Robertson paused expecting to see a reaction, any reaction from Tom. He was disappointed.

"After you mentioned the missing key ring trinket to your DI, Campbell's home was revisited, and this item was analysed and was found to have your DNA on it. What do you have to say about that?"

Again, Tom gave no noticeable reaction.

"And most recently, following a forensic examination of Leanne Young, your DNA was found on her person, specifically a trace was found under her fingernails."

Tom was horrified. It was plausible for someone to plant the key ring and the button, but how on earth could his DNA get under a victim's fingernails unless he was there?

"What size shoe do you wear Tom?" Robertson asked.

"Eight," Tom said in a soft voice.

"I'm sorry Tom, could you say that a bit louder," Reynolds asked.

"Eight," Tom over-emphasised. He knew where he was leading with this question.

"Lastly, Tom," Robertson asked as he slid a single sheet of paper enclosed in a sealed evidence bag onto the table between them, "do you know what this is?"

"Yes," Tom said as he nodded.

"Please tell us what it is," Robertson replied.

At this point Reid leant in and whispered into Tom's ear, he was suggesting that Tom declined to answer this question. Robertson couldn't hear what was being said, all he saw was Tom shake his head as a result of whatever had been said. Despite Reid's advice, Tom answered the question.

"I was factoring the similarities between my previous cases and what had been going on recently, I thought someone was maybe trying to stitch me up."

Robertson chuckled as he sat back in his chair.

"Stitch you up? Is that the defence you're going for, that all this is some elaborate scheme to implicate poor innocent Tom Draven as being a vicious psychopath?" Robertson paused. "Do you know what I think this is? I think this shows the premeditation of a deranged killer. I think this shows you picking your targets *and* your methods before enacting them out to satisfy some twisted lust or fantasy."

"Speak to DI Kilpatrick for Christ's sake," exclaimed Tom interrupting Robertson. "I went to him *immediately* after having seen commonalities forming."

"Ah yes, DI Kilpatrick, yes, he took you off the Burgess case because he found your conclusions highly questionable and didn't want you on an active investigation. Does that sound about right?"

Tom knew he couldn't challenge what had just been said, although what Robertson said was exactly right, he had grossly exaggerated the conversation Tom had had with his DI, but he felt now wasn't an appropriate time to offer a challenge. So, he kept quiet.

Robertson looked over at Reynolds, Reynolds nodded.

"Do you have anything you want to add or clarify at this time, Tom?" Robertson asked.

Tom shook his head.

"Okay." Robertson checked his watch and looked at the clock on the wall. "The time by the interview room clock is eight forty-seven p.m., this interview is over."

Following the interview, Tom was taken back to his cell. It was late, he'd had a long day, and he was tired. It wasn't long after he laid down that he fell asleep.

DAY 15

The hatch in the cell door dropped. A pair of eyes viewed the sleeping body on the bed.

"Do you want any breakfast?" a voice asked.

A face appeared from beneath a blanket and stared at the eyes through the hatch, before again burying itself beneath the blanket. The hatch clanged shut.

A short while later the hatch opened again. A different pair of eyes peered through.

"Are you all right in there?" enquired a voice.

There was no response.

"Oi," was called out, this echoed around the cell, and possibly half of the cell block.

Movement was seen from the body shrouded by a blanket. As that was all that was needed to be observed, the hatch slammed shut again.

As there was no means to determine the passage of time from within the cell it was impossible to know just how much time had passed between visits.

Footsteps could be heard in the corridors, keys heard jangling and turning in other locks. The hatches dropping with calls to check on the welfare of those entrapped within.

Again, the hatch dropped before a key was turned in the lock and the door opened. No response from within. The detention officer entered the cell to rouse the prisoner with gentle persuasion.

The detention officer leant down to shake the prisoner by the foot whilst keeping at a safe distance to prevent being kicked.

He shook the prisoner, who stirred, woke, and looked at him.

"I need you to come to the bridge, you've got a review," the Detention officer said.

The police can hold a prisoner for up to twenty-four hours before they have to charge them with a crime or release them. They can apply for an extension to hold the prisoner up to thirty-six or ninety-six hours if the arrest was made for a serious crime, for example murder. Under the Terrorism Act the prisoner can be held up to fourteen days without charge.

After the first twenty-four hours of detention, a superintendent's review would be required in order to have detention extended initially by another twelve hours. This was that first review as the first twenty-four hours was almost up.

"C'mon, we gotta go," the detention officer emphasised. He was making eye contact with the prisoner, he was definitely being heard, but he was not being understood.

"We've got to go *now.*"

"Nie wiem, co mówisz, nie mówię po angielsku," came the eventual reply from the prone prisoner lying in front of him.

"What the fuck!" exclaimed the detention officer. He was stunned at what had just happened, however he was used to foreign prisoners and how to get them to do what was needed of them.

"I need" — he pointed to himself — "you" — he pointed at the prisoner — "to follow me now." And he pointed out of the door.

The prisoner nodded and stood up.

The detention officer stepped back out of the cell and indicated in which direction he needed the prisoner to walk. detention officers were trained never to lead a prisoner as this made them vulnerable to an attack from behind. They always had to have the prisoner lead the way.

The detention officer showed the prisoner the way back to the bridge where the custody sergeant and a superintendent were waiting for him.

"You're not gonna believe this, Sarge," said the detention officer as he left the prisoner with the officers.

"Mister Draven, I am Superintendent Barlow. As your first twenty-four hours of detention is nearly over I have to do a review of the investigation and decide whether there is justifiable reason to extend your detention."

"Nie wiem, co mówisz, nie mówię po angielsku," came the reply from the prisoner.

The superintendent looked confused, the custody sergeant looked confused. This is not what they were expecting.

There was a moment of silence.

"Is this a game you're playing, Draven? If it is, stop it now," said Barlow.

The prisoner stood there, silent.

"Well, I haven't got a clue what he's saying. If he's playing a game, then let's play it."

"We'll have to use the translator service then, but I haven't got a clue what language it is," said the sergeant.

"It's Polish," said another one of the detention officers.

A look of disbelief crossed the faces of those on duty. They knew who this prisoner was, and no one was expecting this.

The prisoner stood calmly at the bridge whilst a translator was arranged by phone. They would then have a three-way conversation via speakerphone until this charade was over.

"Hello, I am Sergeant Mead, please can you translate my questions and the responses given?"

Having received the response, he wanted Mead to put the phone on loudspeaker and asked the translator to introduce himself to the prisoner.

"Can you ask why he's speaking Polish please?" Mead began.

"Dlaczego mówisz po polsku?" the translator asked.

"Bo jestem Polakiem, nie mówię po angielsku," came the reply.

"Because he *is* Polish, and he doesn't speak English," came the translation.

A sudden hush came over the custody suite. All eyes were on the prisoner. Mead looked at him incredulously. He had witnessed prisoners displaying similar tactics during his career, but in his experience, it never altered the outcome, so he was puzzled why a police officer under arrest would behave in such a way. Resigning himself to this nonsense, Mead sighed.

"Please can you ask him his name?" asked Mead.

"Jak masz na imię?"

"Tomasz Dravidas," came the reply.

"Can you ask him who Tom Draven is please?" Mead was getting concerned and frustrated in equal measures.

"Możesz mi powiedzieć kto Tom Draven jest proszę?"

"Przykro mi, że nie znam nikogo o nazwie Tom Draven," Dravidas replied.

"Um, he doesn't know anyone called Tom Draven," the translator said.

The silence continued.

The sergeant signalled to a detention officer to keep an eye on Dravidas, whilst he and the superintendent stepped into a side office.

"It doesn't matter what his name is or where he's from, he's been linked forensically to the scenes. So, let him play his bloody stupid games. I'll authorise the extension, get a translator in for the interview and let's get this done," Barlow said. "I dunno what he's playing at, but he's a bloody fool if he thinks he can sidestep this with stupid games."

Mead nodded his agreement. "Also, he's remarkably calm for someone who's supposedly just woken up in a cell with allegedly no idea why he's here."

This hadn't occurred to Barlow, but he nodded his approval of this theory. They both then left the side office and resumed their positions in front of the prisoner.

Mead then had to use the translator on the phone to explain to Dravidas why he was arrested, his rights and entitlements and that his extended detention had been authorised. The custody record showed that this had been explained when he was first brought in, but in light of the recent revelation, Mead felt it best to cover it all again.

The translator was also used to ask Dravidas if he wanted any food or drink, which he declined. He was then taken back to his cell.

"You'd better inform Reynolds and Robertson of this as well," Barlow said to Mead before leaving the custody suite.

oOo

DI Reynolds was sitting at his desk when his phone rang.

The detention officer relayed the details of the morning's events.

Reynolds' eyes were wide open in disbelief. In all his years of service, he had never encountered anything like this.

He had been involved in investigating and prosecuting fellow officers for misconduct and suchlike. Usually, they would deny the allegations until such time as overwhelming evidence was presented to them, then they would usually make a full and frank admission.

What he was faced with here was unique for two reasons: Firstly, he had never investigated a fellow officer on suspicion of murder, and also never had the officer under investigation pretended to be someone else to avoid being investigated.

The call was brief as there wasn't a great deal of information to pass on. It ended with Reynolds asking of the detention officer, "Are you able to give DS Robertson a call and tell him the same, can you also ask him to do some digging under the name he's given us?"

The call ended. Reynolds sat back in his chair and spun it round to now face the window.

It was a bright sunny day, he squinted when the brightness hit his face. He closed his eyes momentarily.

"What the fuck is he playing at?"

After a short moment of staring out of the window, Reynolds felt he should seek advice from the superintendent on duty. Given the shift rotation, it may no longer be Barlow, but they should still be updated as to this revelation. Reynolds was already of the opinion that the twelve-hour extension may not be sufficient and wanted to make an early suggestion for a further extension.

Should a further extension to the prisoner's period of detention be required, it would be for the officer in charge of the investigation to make representations to the local magistrates' court, where detention could be extended for up to four days from the time the prisoner first reaches custody of the investigating force.

This last point regarding the investigating force is particularly relevant if the arrest is made elsewhere in the country or overseas. The detention clock doesn't start until the prisoner reaches the investigating force, as it could take a number of days for the prisoner to be transferred or even extradited.

However, an application to the magistrates' court would only be needed if there was a necessity to keep the prisoner in custody without charge. In this case, the evidence to potentially charge with the offence was there. The phone call to the superintendent was seen to be nothing more than a courtesy at this time.

oOo

There was a knock on the DI's door and DS Robertson walked in.

Before he had even stopped walking, Robertson started speaking, "There's no trace of him *anywhere*, not with those details anyway, he's yanking our chain, God knows what his game is."

Robertson sat down and placed some printed pages on the DI's desk.

"I've checked PNC, Interpol and Schengen, nothing; a Tomasz Dravidas doesn't exist with that date of birth."

The Police National Computer (PNC) is a computer system used extensively by forces across the United Kingdom. It went live in 1974 and now consists of several databases available twenty-four hours a day.

The International Criminal Police Organisation (ICPO or Interpol) is an intergovernmental organisation facilitating international police cooperation. It was established as the International Criminal Police Commission (ICPC) in 1923. It chose Interpol as its telegraphic address in 1946 and made it its common name in 1956.

The second-generation Schengen Information System (SISII) allows member European states to raise and respond to alerts in respect of persons, vehicles and objects. The system is used by police, border police, customs officers and other law enforcement authorities. The system is in operation in twenty-four EU member states and four non-EU countries.

"So, what's his game then?" Reynolds replied, "it doesn't matter who he is or what his name is, as things stand he's gonna be charged with at least the attempted murder of Young."

"I've just got off the phone with custody to give 'em the same update, he's still spouting Polish, doesn't respond to a word of English. Keeps buzzing the intercom asking for a fucking fag. From what we know about Draven, he doesn't smoke, quit a few weeks back."

"So fucking what? If I'd quit and was facing a murder charge I think I'd start up again," Reynolds replied, "are we ready to go back in there? What time is the translator arriving?"

"Custody said within the hour, we may as well start heading back down there."

"Okay, let's get this done," Reynolds said, groaning as he stood. He ushered Robertson back towards the door. He grabbed his coat from the coat stand near to the door and put one arm through the first sleeve, grabbing the door handle and closed the door as the second arm went into the other sleeve.

Reynolds straightened his collar as he walked behind Robertson as they both exited the office.

As predicted, by the time they reached the custody suite again the translator had arrived.

They had taken longer than normal to get there as they had grabbed a coffee and a sandwich along the way. They both knew the appalling state of the coffee available at the custody suite, and that chances were that they would be there for a long time. They both resented Draven for that.

When they entered the booking-in area they could see their prisoner back at the desk. A suited male stood next to him. He was balding and wore glasses, and for all intents and purposes looked like a school teacher nearing retirement.

Once again, the force had afforded the prisoner the courtesy of him being the only prisoner out of his cell at that time given his fairly unique status. They didn't want a police officer being seen as a prisoner in front of other detainees.

Because the custody staff felt as if they were now dealing with a new person who had absolutely no recollection of being booked in, the custody sergeant had taken the precaution of essentially booking the prisoner in again with the help of the translator.

Reynolds and Robertson entered to hear the circumstances of arrest being explained.

"You were arrested at your home address having been forensically linked to the attempted murder of Leanne Young on the eighth of February. You were also arrested on suspicion of the murder of Ronald Campbell in Chesterton on second February and the murder of Pauline Barnes in Five Oaks on seventeenth January."

The translator then scribbled some notes, and after a short pause he said, "Został Pan zatrzymany na domowy adres o śledczych związana z usiłowanie zabójstwa Leanne Young ósmego lutego. Możesz również aresztowano na podejrzenie zabójstwa Ronald Campbell w Chesterton drugiego lutego i zabójstwo Pauline Barnes w Five Oaks na XVII stycznia."

The prisoner, understanding what had just been said to him, nodded his response.

"Can you ask him to confirm his name and date of birth?"

"Co to jest imię i nazwisko oraz Data urodzenia?"

"Tomasz Dravidas," the prisoner replied, "20 czerwca 1937."

"Tomasz Dravidas, 20th June 1937," the translator replied.

"20th June 1937," the custody sergeant repeated back to Dravidas. "You're eighty years old? Bollocks, what's your *real* date of birth?"

The translator then repeated the question.

"20 czererwca 1937 roku. To jest moja Data urodzenia," came the reply.

"That *is* his date of birth," the translator confirmed.

"Fine," relented the custody sergeant, "let's just get this done."

With the booking-in completed for the second time, Dravidas was given the option to speak with a solicitor or legal representative prior to being interviewed.

He declined, and when asked to give a reason he stated, "Wiem, co zrobiłem, wydaje się, aby zobaczyć, co zrobiłem jako błędne, ale zrobiłem ten świat lepszym miejscem poprzez usunięcie tych ludzi od niego."

The custody sergeant looked to the translator to enlighten him.

"He says," the translator began, "I know what I've done, you seem to see what I've done as being wrong, but I've made this world a better place by removing these people from it."

A hush fell over the suite. The custody sergeant, along with Reynolds and Robertson stood gobsmacked.

"Oh, my fuckin' good God," Reynolds muttered under his voice, "he's just fucking confessed, I fucking hope the CCTV got all that."

"Yeah, but confessed to what?" Robertson replied, unaware if he should have heard what was muttered.

"He's all yours, sir," the custody sergeant said to Reynolds.

As Dravidas had declined any legal representation there was no need to delay the interview for any consultation, he had also declined meeting with a representative of the Police Federation. Although they had been advised of this turn of events.

Robertson descended the steps that led from the raised area behind the booking-in desks and approached where Dravidas stood with the translator.

Robertson made an introduction as if he were meeting the person standing in front of him for the first time. Reynolds did the same. Once translated and responded to, Robertson led the way to the interview room.

Regardless of the fact that they believed they were essentially interviewing the same person for a second time, they erred on the side of caution and made the introduction as if they were speaking to someone for the first time. Once that was done, the questioning could begin.

It was a lengthy and time-consuming process; Robertson would ask a question, the translator would translate, Dravidas would voice a reply, which would then have to be translated back into English for Robertson and Reynolds' understanding.

One thing became painfully clear to the two detectives, and that was that the man in front of them, in fact, could not speak and did not understand a single word of English. Less than any Polish native resident in the UK. There wasn't the slightest acknowledgement of any of the things being asked of him until they had been translated.

They had done their best to play along believing it to be a well-rehearsed charade, one in which Draven was portraying this persona for whatever reason or whatever gain, but as time went on they found they were speaking to a completely different person.

The body language and mannerisms were completely different to the man that had been sitting across from them the previous day.

The previous day, Draven appeared genuinely oblivious to the details being revealed to him. He couldn't account for the times and dates enquired about, and locations mentioned he stated he had no knowledge of. But what he did have knowledge of – the size eight shoe prints, the missing button and the key ring trinket that turned up at murder scenes – he readily shared what he knew.

Today was different. In appearance he was the same person, although using a different name, he was now sitting across from them appearing not to have a care in the world. He looked relaxed, and casually seemed to be admiring the décor of the interview room between giving comprehensive responses to the questions as they were asked.

However, Dravidas wasn't going to make Robertson or Reynolds' job any easier. His answers were as cryptic and elusive as they were comprehensive.

"What can you tell me about the attempted murder of Leanne Young?" Robertson asked.

The translator had to ask Dravidas to pause several times, so he could scribble some notes. This was the only aspect of the interview process that appeared to frustrate Dravidas.

The translator began reciting his reply, "I know her, she's a prostitute, a spreader of disease, you'll see, she was bitter, infected and vengeful, she wanted to spread her disease to as many as she could. Go on, ask in her circles, they'll tell you."

"How did your DNA get under her fingernails?"

The translator translated.

"Prawdopodobnie ponieważ chciała, aby zainfekować mnie zbyt, I położyć kres do tego," replied Dravidas.

"He says probably because she wanted to infect me too, I put a stop to that," the translator said.

Dravidas held up both forearms with the back of his hands towards where Reynolds and Robertson sat.

They could see evidence of fresh abrasion injuries, consistent with having been caused by fingernail scratches.

"Did you try to kill her?" Reynolds added.

Dravidas replied, then the translator said, "I wanted to do what was necessary to stop her spreading disease and causing misery."

After more questions and more note taking on Young the questioning moved onto Campbell.

"Did you kill Ronald Campbell?"

Again, the translated response was cryptic. "I've stopped him causing harm, you'll see."

Dravidas answered all the questions both Reynolds and Robertson had for him, except one.

He was asked about the Lego mini-figure key ring.

This was the only time that a look of confusion came across his face.

"Nie mam pojęcia, co ty gadasz," Dravidas said.

"Um, he doesn't know what you're talking about," came the translation.

Similarly, when the questions moved onto that of Barnes. Dravidas again had no recollection of the button that had been found at the scene.

Reynolds opened the questioning. "Tomasz, I can see where you're coming from when it comes to Young and Campbell, you feel you needed to kill them to prevent them from harming others, but surely you didn't feel similarly towards Pauline

Barnes?" He paused. "A divorced mother of two, what risk did she pose to society?"

The translator translated.

"Widocznie nie zrobiłeś swoją pracę domową na jej," Dravidas replied.

"He says evidently you've not done your homework on her," the translator said.

A puzzled look fell across the faces of Reynolds and Robertson. This confusion was in turn felt by the translator.

Seeing their confusion Dravidas added to his response, "Nie trzeba kopać bardzo głęboko, aby zobaczyć, co mam na myśli."

There was a pause before the translator realised all eyes were on him to do his job.

"Um, do some digging, you'll see what he means."

When the time came to question Dravidas on the death of Callum Burgess they had been in the interview for almost two hours.

Had Dravidas asked for a break they would have paused the interview, but Reynolds and Robertson were not going to interrupt the process for their benefit.

Robertson introduced the change of topic by giving a brief overview of the Burgess investigation and crime scene.

Whilst the questions were being asked it became apparent that Dravidas' attention was elsewhere.

The translator had to gain his attention before offering the translation.

"Jestem coraz głodny teraz, nic więcej dzisiaj," he eventually said.

"He says he's hungry, no more today he says," the translator said.

Robertson looked across to Reynolds, Reynolds turned his written notes, so Robertson could see them. He nodded his understanding.

"Okay, Tomasz, you're gonna be charged with the attempted murder of Leanne Young and the murders of Ronald Campbell and Pauline Barnes, is there anything you want to add or clarify?" Robertson said.

Once translated Tomasz shook his head.

"This interview is over, the time is 5:12 p.m."

Robertson exited the interview room to see if the booking-in area was clear to bring Dravidas out.

He returned after a moment and beckoned to his DI who led Dravidas back out to the booking-in area.

A detention officer took charge of Dravidas and started to lead him back to his cell.

"He wants something to eat," Robertson called across to the detention officer.

Reynolds was in discussion with the custody sergeant. "He's gonna be charged with two murders and the attempt."

"Did he admit to them then?" The custody sergeant enquired.

"Not exactly, but we've got enough to charge."

From this moment, the detention clock would stop. Dravidas would remain in police detention until he was collected by the company responsible for the transportation and security of prisoners between custody and court.

Dravidas would now face an initial hearing where he could enter a plea before being either sent for trial or sentencing.

Until then he would face another night in police detention.

DAY 16

The day started exactly the same as the previous day when the hatch dropped open. A face then appeared, at a distance at first, then once the prisoner was seen to be at a safe distance away from the door on the bench they closed in and all that could be seen were a pair of eyes.

"Good morning," the detention officer said.

The figure on the bed stirred at being address. He rolled over to respond to the voice. Looking towards the cell door he sat up, stretching and rotating joints until an eased and comfortable posture was found.

"Morning," came the confused reply, "what's going on?"

The detention officer had been told what could await him when he attended the cell. He was told he may not be understood verbally due to the possibility of a language barrier.

As a result, he now looked as confused as the prisoner.

There was a long pause. Then eventually the detention officer broke the silence, "Do you want some breakfast?" and began to list the options available.

"Sausage and beans please," came the reply as if he were well versed in the custody menu, as his selection had yet to be mentioned.

The complete menu was limited. Microwaveable meals and the added option of cereal and a Pot-Noodle type snack meal. Because of the limited options available it wasn't unheard of for prisoners to request a curry or chilli for breakfast.

The eyes dropped out of sight momentarily as the detention officer scribbled the request on a notepad. "Tea or coffee?"

"Coffee, please," came the reply.

The hatch closed.

oOo

A short while later a breakfast of sausage and beans and a coffee was served, which had to be eaten indignantly with a *spork,* the unholy lovechild of a spoon and a fork which serves the role of neither.

During breakfast, the custody sergeant attended the cell. He dropped the inspection hatch and addressed the prisoner.

"Good morning." Then after receiving an acknowledgement of a grunted reply whilst consuming a mouthful of beans he continued, "Can I ask you to confirm your name, please?"

There was a moment of silence as the prisoner cleared his mouth to be able to verbalise a response. He felt that the custody sergeant had intentionally timed his request to coincide with a mouthful. Rather like sitting in a restaurant when the waiting staff wait for you to take that mouthful before asking "Is everything ok?". They seem never to attend at any other time.

Once free to respond the reply came.

"Thomas Draven," he said, "and would you mind telling me what the fuck is going on here?"

The custody sergeant checked the corridor for any other prisoners being escorted around the suite before unlocking the cell door. Once the door was open he took a couple of steps inside.

"You've been charged and remanded for the offences that you were arrested for. You are awaiting transport to court shortly."

"What's happened since I've been here?" Draven asked.

"I haven't got time to go into detail with that" — the custody sergeant paused — "but as you know your defence can get a copy of the custody record."

Having been denied a direct answer Draven ground his teeth for a moment. He then gave the custody sergeant a stare; a stare that unnerved the sergeant to such an extent that he immediately and hastily took two big steps backwards and out of the cell before shutting the door with a loud and echoing slam. Once behind the safety of the door, he ventured a peek through the still opened hatch. Draven could see the fear in his eyes before he finally closed the hatch.

There was, albeit for only a moment, a time when he felt that he was at risk of losing control. He felt something he had never felt before, an uncontrollable energy rising within him. An energy that would've manifested itself in him potentially launching himself at the custody sergeant. Luckily, the sergeant with all his years of experience saw the warning signs and retreated from harm's way in the nick of time. Following that there was a moment of clarity. "What the fuck was that about?" he muttered to himself.

It was an irrational reaction as the sergeant had given him a positive response. The custody record contains a detailed chronological sequence of all events and interactions with a prisoner during their time in custody including all welfare checks on the prisoner in his cell during the rest period. This is to include any moods or anger noted, any dialogue or requests, and should they be asleep, it would have to include the position they were asleep in and that movement and/or breathing was noted.

This would therefore indirectly answer Draven's question without the custody sergeant having to respond whilst under the watchful eye of the in-cell AV (audio/visual) CCTV.

After Draven had finished his breakfast he was given the opportunity to take a shower, which he declined. His reasoning was that he would be putting back on the same clothes that he had worn for the last two days. He felt he knew where this was heading. Even without the benefit of viewing the custody record, he was beginning to piece together what was happening to him. He knew that he had been arrested on suspicion of two murders and an attempted murder, and the custody sergeant confirmed in the cell that he had been charged with those offences. Draven knew that he wasn't going to be going home any time soon.

The cell door opened, a different detention officer appeared in the open doorway holding up Draven's shoes. "Time to go," he said.

Tom stood up from the bench and walked out of the cell. This time the cell door had been pushed back as far as it would go, as the cell would now need to be cleaned and checked before the next guest.

As before, Tom was requested to lead the way back to the booking-in area.

Behind the desk was the same sergeant as earlier. He looked calmer now than when Tom had last seen him. In front at the counter were two large men in a different uniform. Tom instantly realised that they would be from the prisoner courier service.

Tom approached the desk to be addressed by the sergeant.

"Thomas Draven, you are being charged with three offences, that on the seventeenth of January in Five Oaks you murdered Pauline Barnes, that on the second of February in Chesterton you murdered Ronald Campbell, and finally that on the eighth February at Southfields you attempted to murder Leanne Young."

After the charges were read out to Tom he was given a chance to reply to them. He said nothing, he just stared straight ahead defiantly. Almost oblivious to the proceedings.

This moment of reflection was interrupted by one of the transport officers speaking to him. The comment was heard but no response was given.

"Oi!" was bellowed at close proximity to Tom's ear, so that he had no choice but to hear it.

Tom turned to face the transport officer. He initially only turned his head in order to face him, then followed by rotating the rest of his body to stand squarely in front of him.

Tom looked at him, looked through him with the same piercing stare that he had given the custody sergeant a short time before.

"You can wipe that look off your face as soon as you like, sonny," the transport officer said, "you don't scare me, I've seen it all before."

The booking-in area fell quiet. All eyes were on Tom. The custody sergeant had now stood up and was slowly walking around the desks to be near to where Tom was standing.

"Hold out your hands," the transport officer said sternly. He was about the make the request for a second time when he saw Tom's hands come up between them, loosely closed fists with wrists a couple of inches apart.

Tom knew the drill, he'd been cuffed countless times in training. Common police practice was to handcuff a prisoner in what is known as a *front stack* position, which is essentially with the arms in a folded position and using rigid bar cuffs. He knew that the transport officers only use chain linked cuffs, so a stack position wouldn't be possible due to the rotation of the chain links.

The transport officer cuffed Tom's hands together. He then took a second set of cuffs, one of which was already attached to his own right wrist around a thick leather padded bracer, and cuffed Tom to him.

The bracer was there in case the prisoner resisted or in any way pulled on the officer's arm. The bracer would protect his arm and the cuffs would then cause the prisoner more pain than the officer.

Tom was then led from the custody suite to a waiting prison van which was in the secure loading dock. Once inside the van, Tom was sitting inside a cell. The specially modified door was then closed. The modification allowed for Tom to still be cuffed to the officer. Only once secured in the cell did the officer then release Tom from the second set of cuffs that attached Tom to him.

The dock doors opened, and the van slowly pulled out into the morning sunshine. Tom hadn't seen natural light for over two days. Even now his brief glimpse of it was through heavily tinted windows.

oOo

"Fucking hell!" DS Robertson exclaimed. He was reviewing his notes on the Draven/Dravidas interview and performing some background checks to elaborate on what had been said. Specifically, the background checks were being performed on the victims of the murders.

"Fucking hell, *what?*" came the reply when no further exclamation was forthcoming.

"Barnes, um, Pauline Barnes, she wasn't as squeaky clean as we thought. That murdering bastard was on to something."

Robertson clicked on the print icon on his desktop computer and then went over to the printer to await his document.

Once it was printed he came back to his desk and taking a fluorescent yellow highlighter pen highlighted the salient points he would need to refer back to.

Once the printed document was ready Robertson took it to his inspector's office. The door was open, but as he peeked around the door he saw the inspector, Inspector Tickner, was on the phone. He was working because Reynolds was on leave. The inspector saw him. He held up a single finger suggesting it was a short call and that Robertson should wait where he was.

When the call ended, Robertson heard, "Come in have a seat," come from within the office.

Robertson entered the office and took a seat. After making himself comfortable he started speaking.

"Good morning, sir," he began, "I've been doing some background checks on what came from the Draven interview yesterday."

"Ah yes, Reynolds gave me an overview of what happened, started speaking Polish or something mid-way through his detention. What's that all about?"

"I'm not sure, sir, surprised the hell out of me, it was like we were interviewing two different people over the two days, neither having a clue about the other it seemed."

"What have you got for me then," the DI asked.

"Well, sir, as you know Draven denied everything. Well, he admitted being at the scene of the Burgess killing, and that he was invited to the Campbell scene, but denied everything else. But the other guy…" Robertson paused to find the name from his notes. "…Dravidas, said we had more to find out about the so-called victims. Well, I've done some digging and found some very surprising stuff."

"So, what have you found then?" There seemed to be some urgency behind the inspector's request, as if to hurry Robertson along to make his point.

"Well, sir, first of all, Campbell wasn't the reformed character we thought he was. There are reports of continued offending consistent with his previous convictions involving children. Nothing as far as charging goes, but there are a number of investigations up and down the country where his name keeps coming up."

"Oh, okay, well that's hardly front-page news that a child sex offender continues to be a child sex offender, now is it?" Tickner exclaimed matter-of-factly.

"No, sir, but what I found out about Barnes is more startling."

"Barnes, which one is Barnes?" Tickner asked.

"She's the one who was stabbed in the back of the head in the car park, sir. Up until now, we all thought she was squeaky clean, y'know the butter-wouldn't-melt-in-her-mouth type thing. Well, it turns out she's not so squeaky clean. She's a domiciliary carer, sir, end of life care. Well, a couple of years ago there was an investigation into her being less than caring. She was cleared from the police investigation, but the family of a deceased client tried for a private prosecution which again led nowhere. They've remained resolute that she was responsible for a premature death. And because nothing was ever proven she's remained working, granted she's moved around a bit, but she's still working."

"Bloody hell," replied Tickner, "so how would Draven know about this?"

"Well, sir, according to him, he doesn't, it was Dravidas who said we should do some digging on her. If it wasn't for that I wouldn't have looked."

"Well, Draven's in the job, so if you could find out then so could he," Tickner replied. "Is Barnes currently under any kind of investigation?"

"Not currently by any police force, but I have gone out to her current employer for her work record and details of any previous employment to make contact with them."

"Okay, kick over all the stones you can, come back to me when you get a response."

"Yessir," Robertson said. He stood up and left the office.

oOo

"All rise," said the court usher.

Tom rose to his feet as the court came into session. He was required to confirm his name and date of birth for the benefit of the court.

The court session today consisted of the magistrate, the clerk of the court who was the legally trained advisor to the court, and the prosecutor. Tom did not feel the need to be represented at this hearing as it was only to enter his plea.

Murder is an indictable offence, so he would be committed for trial or sentencing at the Crown Court. This hearing would allow the Crown Court to be advised whether a full trial by jury would be required or whether a sentencing hearing would be all that is required.

The charges, identical to what had been read out by the custody sergeant earlier that morning, were read out before the court.

"On these charges, how do you plead?" the magistrate asked.

"Not guilty, Your Honour," Tom said with conviction.

There was a pause whilst the clerk approached the bench. They were seen to deliberate for a few moments before the clerk went back to his bench.

The magistrate cleared his throat before addressing the court. "You have entered a plea of not guilty, trial date has been set to commence on Monday May 31st. You will be remanded in custody until such time. Do you have anything you wish to say?"

Tom shook his head.

The sound of the gavel coming down echoed throughout the courtroom. Tom jumped as its sound broke the moment of silence that preceded it.

The magistrate and the clerk filed out of the courtroom. Court detention officers then led Tom back down to the holding area where he would await ongoing transportation.

He knew there was a HMPS prison nearby which would be the normal logical choice for prisoners on remand in this locality. However, there was nothing normal about this situation. Tom felt confident they weren't about the stick a cop in the general population of a prison.

What were they going to do with him? Only time would tell.

DAY 17

Following the initial court hearing, Tom was returned to the detention cells below the court.

He had to be kept there overnight. Tom was still a special case. However, what was happening should not have come as a surprise to anyone, yet nothing had been prepared. As there were no catering facilities, food had to be ordered in for him.

May the 31st was over three months away. Under normal circumstances, a remanded prisoner would spend this time in prison, and this time would be deducted from any future sentence imposed.

But these were not normal circumstances. Tom was not a normal prisoner. These factors should have been anticipated and factored into decisions already made, but they weren't.

As a result, he ended up spending the rest of the day of the initial hearing and the next day in the court's holding cells before a course of action was eventually put into effect.

However, by this time the prisoner was no longer in a position to understand what was being asked of him, and with no translator available the court staff did their best by using translation apps on their smartphones to make themselves understood.

It was Tomasz who was transported to a category B prison. This was mercifully not the local one, but one that was a three-hour drive away.

This prison, in particular, was probably decided upon to minimise the chances of anyone in the general population recognising Tom as a police officer. If this information was known to the general population then it could prove troublesome for all concerned and could put Tom in potentially grave danger.

The prison governor was aware of the unique status of his new prisoner; however, it was left to his discretion whether or not to disseminate this to his staff. He chose not to.

There were days when the new prisoner was happy to blend into the shadows and keep his head down. Doing anything and everything not to draw any attention to himself. Then there were other days when the same prisoner would be jostling for position in the meal queues and doing his utmost to antagonise fellow inmates.

He would constantly frustrate them by insulting them in a language they didn't understand.

This prisoner was going out of his way to make sure the whole wing knew he was there.

DAY 29

"So, a little birdie tells me the new fish is a pig," a deep voice whispered in Tom's ear as he was waiting in the queue in the mess hall, "is that what you is, fish, a pig?"

Tom turned to see a mountain of a man standing directly behind him. The top of Tom's head was level with the man's chin.

Tom didn't say a word, he knew that anything he could say in such a situation would be the wrong thing.

"Hey, pig-fish, is that you? Y'know I could shout that out and everyone would hear it, and you wouldn't survive the fucking night."

Tom could feel his heart about to explode out of his chest it was beating so fast.

The man-mountain leant in forward and whispered so only Tom could hear him, "You're mine, pig-fish, having a pet pig-fish could be useful."

Tom could only manage the slightest of nods to show his understanding. The man-mountain then pushed ahead of Tom in the queue.

Tom had suddenly lost his appetite. As he went to replace his tray in the stack he heard another voice speak from behind him, "What did he say to you?"

"He called me fish, told me I was his," Tom replied as he turned to see an ageing black prisoner standing behind him. He was holding his full tray having been served and was heading to sit down when he witnessed the altercation.

"Sit with me," he said, "I'll educate you about a few things around here." He then nodded with his head in the direction of a free bench table away from the masses.

As Tom followed him he heard him say, "This don't make us friends, fish, you still a fish, and me and you ain't buddies, you get me. We'll never sit together again, and don't speak to me unless I speak to you first."

Tom felt cautious, but he felt he had no choice, he needed to get an education on life on the inside. They sat out of earshot of anyone.

"What's your name then, fish?" he asked.

"I'm Tom," came the reply.

"First time inside, Tom?"

Tom nodded.

"I'm Wilson." He paused to take a mouthful of what was probably meant to resemble a shepherd's pie or lasagne. "Well, you've got a lot to learn, Tom. Looks like you're quickly making friends. What are you in for?"

"Remand until trial. Who is that guy?" Tom asked.

"That's Baxter," Wilson replied, "he's someone you don't want to fuck with, and he's certainly someone whose shit list you don't wanna be on. He's a mean motherfucker, and he'll end you if you fuck with him. What you s'posed to have done then?"

"Two and a half murders," Tom said, "I don't plan to, believe you me, I plan to stay well out of his way from now on."

"Why the half?" Wilson asked.

"Last one didn't die," Tom replied.

Wilson smiled and gave a nod of approval.

"Staying out of his way won't make any difference now, he's made a claim on you, he owns you now, you'd best be at his beck and call from now on, coz if he has to go looking for you, he'll make you sorry he did."

"Fucking hell," Tom muttered under his breath. That's the last thing he needed. Not only was Baxter the alpha on the wing, somehow, he also knew Tom's secret. He was starting to realise that if he didn't bow to him he was in for a world of pain.

"Any suggestions how I should deal with this?"

"There's no way to deal with this, you his now, plain and simple, guys in here are afraid of him, they won't help you, and after today don't go asking me for help neither. The guys here are just happy that you're the object of his affections and not them, and they've got no intention of changing that."

There was silence as Wilson ate and Tom thought.

"The only thing you can do is get out of here, coz he sure as hell ain't going anywhere. Now fuck off before anyone thinks we're in bed together."

Tom took the hint and rose from his seat. He whispered, "Thanks," to Wilson as he did.

No one seemed to pay him any attention as he left the canteen area, more importantly Baxter was nowhere to be seen. That was probably the only reason Wilson had chosen to speak to him.

Tom realised he knew nothing about Wilson. But Tom was aware of the prison dynamic, and he knew that Wilson had stuck his neck out to even speak to him, and for that he was grateful.

175

DAY 68

"Ohmigod Tom, what's happened to you?"

Jess sat across the table from Tom in the visitor's centre of the prison. The centre itself was a separate building inside the walls of the main prison. Prisoners were brought in through a passage lined with high fences and barbed wire. Visitors entered via a brick-built corridor from the reception area.

"I'm okay, just a little rough and tumble," Tom replied.

"What happened?" asked Jess with increasing concern.

"To be honest I don't even know how most of it happened, yeah, I've had a couple of run-ins with people, it seems I wake up with fresh bruises every other day almost," Tom sniggered. "I seem to be making a lot of friends around here."

He adjusted his posture so as to lean over the table more, and Jess mimicked this action. "To tell you the truth I don't know what's happening here, and no one seems to be able to tell me. It's bizarre, for example, y'know I don't smoke any more, yet I'm finding I've got fags on me virtually every time I wake up, God knows where I'm getting them from? I started giving them away which I thought would put me in good stead with everyone here but no. I'm always finding more on me, along with fresh injuries."

"Tom, you've got to tell the guards," Jess said.

"C'mon, Jess, y'know I can't do that, I've just gotta keep my head down until I get outta here. But this place is so cliché: getting stuck in the queue at meal times and blindsided in the showers."

Tom started to recall the most recent incident for Jess almost as if the narrative would suggest a black and white flashback in a movie.

"It was one evening a couple of weeks ago, the showers and the meals queues are the only places you're really vulnerable. There's no CCTV in the showers, and the mess halls are so crowded you can't really see anything going on. I was only in there for a shave. I felt I was reasonably safe as I could see the room in the mirror and didn't have my back exposed. A couple of guys came in, have seen them on the block and in the mess hall, they were chatting, didn't think that much of it. The

passageway between the rows of basins is enough to drive a bus through yet one was walking unnecessarily close to my side. As he passed I felt cold, cold like an ice cube had been dropped down my back. It was only after they'd gone that I felt something else, like I'd pissed myself. I put my hand back to feel the wetness, and brought it back around the front to see blood. I then turned to show my back to the mirror, it was only then that I saw it. I'd been slashed across the kidneys, luckily it wasn't deep, but deep enough to bleed like a bastard."

During his recollection, he had looked around the visitor's centre. Not to see if anyone was eavesdropping, but because he couldn't face Jess whilst describing these events.

When he did finally make eye contact again with her he could see she had her hands cupped over the lower part of her face and that she was welling up.

"It's a rough place here, worse for me, that much is for sure, I dunno how much longer my secret will stay secret." Tom paused and again had a brief look around the visitor's centre to ensure no one was in earshot of their conversation. "I have spoken to the Guv'nor, he knows my situation, I think he's the only one who does, mind, he also knows that someone else has leaked it. He's a good guy, he's arranging a transfer to another prison for me. This one guy, he's huge, a gigantic bald fucker, he's the one who knows, God knows how, he wants me to be his bitch or he's gonna make it common knowledge; if he does it's gonna be bad news for me. I don't know if these other guys knew it or were just acting on instructions, or that I'd just pissed them off. Either way, I'm not taking any chances. Hopefully, I'll get my transfer before anything worse happens."

Tom could see that Jess was still on the verge of bursting into tears. He knew he should quickly change the subject.

"On the plus side I've lost some weight, I would say I'm eating healthier but that just wouldn't be true. There is a sort of gym here, but I don't go there as that seems to be another place where bad things can happen."

Jess looked at Tom's face, she nodded and smiled at having noticed the change in his face due to his recent weight loss.

"Just stay safe, hun," Jess replied. "How come this is the first time I've got to see you, you've been here for almost two months. I've been here several times, but each time they said you've declined visitation. What's been going on?"

Tom looked puzzled. "Y'know I could say the same thing, I get the visit scheduled then I get told it's been cancelled, and they say I cancelled it, I don't know what the fuck's going on around here."

Tom paused and had another look around.

"Hopefully, I'll be transferred soon. You know I didn't do any of this, don't you?"

"I know," Jess replied vehemently, smiling as she did.

She knew that Tom couldn't possibly have committed the crimes that he was being held for. She felt confident that he would be vindicated in time. But she was worried that he would keep getting fresh injuries whenever she did get to see him.

At the end of the session, Jess stood up to leave. She put her coat back on and stepped away from the table. She wanted to move round to Tom's side to hug him, but as she took a step in his direction she saw a sign on the wall that said *NO PHYSICAL CONTACT BETWEEN VISITORS AND PRISONERS*. She knew this was to prevent the passing of drugs, weapons or mobile phones or SIM cards, but all she wanted to do was hug him.

She sighed. In her disappointment, she recalled a favour she had been asked. "Carl says hi, he says to stay strong. It'll all come out in the end." She paused. "He says he's been banned from coming here himself. Came from above apparently. Bunch of fucking arseholes if you ask me."

Tom smiled. "I thought that'd probably be the case, I'm surprised he was able to get a message to you to pass on."

They both smiled at each other briefly before a female guard stepped forward and ushered Jess towards the exit. As Jess left the room a male guard came and escorted Tom out of a different door, a door that would lead him back inside the walls of the prison.

DAY 77

"*Wydostać się z mojej drodze małego Konia Kutas kurwa,*" could be heard over the shoulder of a bald man-mountain standing in the queue for his lunch.

The same bald man-mountain who had previously been the topic of conversation between Tom and fellow inmate Wilson. That conversation meant that he now had a name, a name that to the normal *cat* or *kanga* came with a sense of trepidation; Aaron Baxter.

Since that conversation, it was revealed that Baxter was in the middle of serving *an eight* for armed robbery. Armed robbery was a respected offence amongst the population as it was inherently violent; they respect violence.

Baxter turned to see Tomasz standing behind him. As before, the little man hardly came up to his chin. He was standing behind him and staring at him, at him and through him.

"What the fuck did you say to me?" he replied as he turned, and upon realising who it was he added, "ah, my little pig-fish."

Tomasz started to poke Baxter in the centre of his chest, right at the base of his sternum.

"You," he said, emphasising this with a poke, "you – fucking – little – horse – dick," he said in broken English and with a distinct Polish accent, and with every word spoken came yet another poke on exactly the same spot.

The English translation was heard and understood far more than the Polish insult that had preceded it. As a result, a silence had fallen over the mess hall. Even the serving staff had downed ladles to see what would happen next.

No one had challenged Baxter since he had been at this prison. Baxter was the undisputed top dog.

The eyes of the room, however, were not on the smaller Polish antagonist, they were on Baxter. They wanted to know how he was going to react to such a public humiliation and challenge. Amongst those watching was Wilson. He could clearly see what was going on but was hidden amongst the crowd that had formed.

Whatever Baxter chose to do, he could not choose to just ignore the insult, or dismiss it and laugh it off. He was being challenged, and the challenge had to be responded to in a way to assert his dominance and quell the thoughts of any likeminded individuals.

Tomasz obviously knew more about Baxter than vice versa. He knew that this guy was the one to throw a power challenge at. He had bided his time since being in prison, he had watched, he had listened, and he had learned.

Tomasz was an unknown entity, he was recognised, but what Baxter was now facing was unfamiliar. Regardless, the challenge was to be automatically accepted. Baxter had no choice in that matter.

He responded on equal terms. He started by poking Tomasz in the chest. Due to the height difference, he was unable to poke him squarely in the sternum as he had received. His finger extended downwards.

"Why don't you just fuck off before you get hurt, little man," was Baxter's opening comeback.

On the poke that coincided with *little man,* Tomasz calmly closed his left hand around the right index finger that was poking him. He held it in a firm grip, but not too tight to cause Baxter to instinctively withdraw his hand.

With the long finger held in the small fist, Baxter's finger extended beyond his fist exposing it to the first knuckle.

Tomasz stepped back extending his left arm so as to keep the finger and his closed hand where it was.

A stunned and puzzled look then came across Baxter's face.

Tomasz then tightened his grip around the finger, at the same moment landing a palm heel strike onto the exposed tip of the finger causing the finger to burst at the first knuckle. Bones were seen to protrude through the skin.

Baxter screamed in agony. But the worst was yet to come.

Tomasz closed the striking hand around the damaged end of the finger and ripped it from the hand. Blood shot from the open wound spraying across Tomasz.

Baxter was stunned. He was in too much pain to resist or even realise what was happening to him.

Because Tomasz was significantly shorter than Baxter the pull was downwards and dragged him down to his knees.

Tomasz then stepped in close and whispered into Baxter's ear before circling around behind him.

"Don't – fuck – with – me."

Tomasz then fed Baxter his own detached digit by ramming it into his mouth before pushing him to the ground. Baxter instinctively put his hands down to cushion his fall, in doing so he landed on his injured hand. His screams of pain echoed across the mess hall.

Tomasz then stood up straight and surveyed the room. He was checking to see if anyone was going to retaliate after what they had just witnessed.

Nothing happened. The room was in silence. No guards could be seen either.

Then in an instant, the room returned to normal as if nothing had happened. Conversations continued and serving resumed.

There were only two things different to how the room was before: there was a man cowering on the floor nursing a severely injured hand, and Baxter was no longer the top dog. He would never come back from such a challenge.

Tomasz calmly left the mess hall with not a word being said to him.

DAY 95

Tom was unaware why the prison politics had suddenly changed. But he certainly wasn't going to argue.

He hadn't seen Baxter for quite some time. He had heard that he had sustained an injury and was being treated in a local hospital before being transferred to another prison.

Tom had been informed that his own transfer would no longer be going ahead due to Baxter having now left the prison. The Warden now knew that it was Baxter who had become aware of Tom's status, and with him gone he felt confident that Tom was no longer at risk.

Another thing Tom had noticed was that other prisoners were now giving him a wide birth. He found he was able to go about the prison unmolested, he was able to keep himself to himself without challenge. This he took solace in, and even enjoyed.

Tom sat on his bunk, his cell door open. His gaze was at his feet, his mind elsewhere.

Then there was a knock on the open door of his cell. The first went ignored, then a few moments later there was a second knock. Normally a second knock would be louder than the first, however this second knock was softer, almost sounding apologetic compared to the first.

Tom looked across towards the open door.

His gaze settled on a young lad standing in the open doorway. He was holding something with both hands and stood in a manner even more apologetic than his second knock suggested.

Tom didn't say a word. This situation was alien to him, he didn't know how to react to it, so he would allow this person to introduce the situation.

Tom maintained his posture and gaze and remained silent, eventually his visitor broke the silence.

He entered the cell and extended both arms towards to Tom, much like Oliver holding his bowl out for 'more.' As he came closer Tom could see what he was holding; two sealed packs of rolling tobacco.

His visitor offered them in such a way that he was expecting Tom to take them. Tom didn't make a move, there was no change to his demeanour, this took a huge effort on his part as he was trying not to look confused by the situation.

The visitor had entered the cell far enough that he was level with the end of the bed. He froze. He had expected some reaction from Tom. He appeared cautious and was desperately trying to judge Tom's mood.

"I'll just leave them here," he said as he delicately laid the tobacco on the end of the bed. He laid them down as gently as if he were laying a sleeping baby back in its cot.

The visitor stood up, and slowly backed out of the cell. Once he had retreated as far as the door to the relative safety of the landing he swiftly turned to his right and disappeared out of sight.

"Wait, WAIT," Tom yelled out. He was off his bed as quick as lightning and across to the cell door. Once out onto the landing he turned to his left expecting to see his visitor halfway down the landing by now. But no, he was standing, almost to attention, just outside the cell. Tom yelling *wait* had brought him to an immediate halt.

This confused Tom even more.

Tom knew he had to pick his words carefully.

"Why did you give me two packets of tobacco?" he asked.

The figure stood before him, making no effort to turn around to face who was addressing him. There was a long pause before a reply came.

"I could only get hold of two, I'm sorry, I'll get you the rest, I'm good for it, just give more time."

"That's not what I meant," Tom paused, he looked around the landing. His outburst had attracted some unwanted attention. He wanted some privacy before entertaining his curiosity. "Come here," he said beckoning his visitor back into his cell.

His visitor felt he had no choice in the matter. But nonetheless, he cautiously turned around. Tom had already re-entered his cell, so he slowly followed.

As he entered he saw Tom standing against the back wall of the cell beneath the window with his arms folded across his chest.

Tom could see that his visitor was looking sheepish and uneasy. But he knew he shouldn't go to any great lengths to undo whatever had happened to change the dynamic around him. But conversely, he did need to get at least some information from the young lad standing in front of him.

"Sit yourself down, mate, I just want to ask you about a few things," Tom said in a relaxed yet authoritative manner. He found it hard to say it any other way, after all, he was still a copper.

The lad sat as he had been instructed to. From where Tom stood he looked like a naughty schoolboy sitting outside the headmaster's office.

The lad felt he needed to provide an explanation. "I could only get two packets, I promise I'll make it up to you next w…"

Tom interrupted him, "I'm not interested in the fucking baccy, okay."

His interruption caused the lad to withdraw even further.

This isn't going well, Tom thought, and realised he needed to rethink his tactics.

He pushed himself away from the wall and joined the lad sitting on the bed. Tom felt this was best as he really didn't want the whole wing hearing what he had to ask of this young lad.

Small steps, he thought. "What's your name?"

"Bryan," came the reply.

"Hello, Bryan, I'm Tom…"

"Tomasz, I know," Bryan replied interrupting Tom in doing so.

Tomasz, Tom had heard that name before. But the repeated mentioning of it did not enlighten him at all.

"So, what's with the baccy?" he asked.

Bryan began to explain to him that a few months earlier *he* had helped him when he had a run in with a few other prisoners, and that they had come to an arrangement whereby Bryan would keep him in tobacco in exchange for Tomasz keeping an eye out for him.

Tom looked at Bryan, he was 130 lbs in his clothes soaking wet, and no taller than he was at five foot eight.

"What are you in for?" Tom felt compelled to ask.

Bryan paused, realising that they'd previously had the same conversation, but he felt compelled to answer regardless, "Drugs."

Tom simply nodded, almost expecting that reply.

"So, why is everyone keeping their distance from me now?" Tom asked feeling he needed to speed the conversation along not knowing how long they had.

"Baxter," Bryan replied matter-of-factly, "what you did to him in the lunch queue."

Bryan could see the confused look on Tom's face. He could see that Tom was doing his best to make sense of what he had just been told, but it was not making any sense to him. Bryan realised he would need to explain it in simpler terms.

"You fed him his own fucking finger in front of everybody, made him choke on the fucking thing."

Things were starting to fall into place for Tom, he'd dreamed that this had taken place and came up with his own reasons why Baxter was hospitalised, but until now nothing had been said to him.

"Why hasn't the Guv'nor spoken to me about it, and why haven't I been nicked?" Tom asked.

"No one likes Baxter, the guy's a fucking wanker, he got what he deserved. No one saw nothing, you get me."

"Go on," Tom said requesting more details.

"The queue was busy, yeah, it was over in a blink, no guards actually saw it, no one came running, no alarms. Yeah, there was some claret but nothing we hadn't seen spilt before."

"And what happened to the finger then?"

"What finger?" Bryan asked.

"The fucking finger that I supposedly fed to him?"

"It's what I'm saying, what finger? After he spits it out someone picks it up and it gets chucked in the chip fryer, don't it." Bryan paused to have a brief chuckle. "So, some poor fucker ends up with it deep fried on their plate, gives a whole new meaning to finger licking good, I s'pose."

Tom got the impression he'd been saving that line up for a while now.

"And no one says a bloody thing, least of all Baxter, last thing he wants is to be a branded as a snitch. He kept his mouth shut, after he spat his finger out that is," Bryan finished with another chuckle.

Still Tom looked perplexed. He thanked Bryan and sent him on his way. He told him not to worry about bringing any more tobacco, that he'd already more than settled any debt.

As Bryan exited the cell he heard Tom say to him, "Stay out of trouble, y'hear, I don't wanna have to come saving your arse again."

Tom was alone in his cell again. He thought back to the last time the name Tomasz had been mentioned to him, by the custody sergeant when he was charged with the murders. But the name didn't make any more sense to him now than it did then.

Day 122

Tom spent the remaining weeks in the prison until his trial date without incident.

He had seen Bryan in the halls a few times since their chat, but they never spoke again. But each time they acknowledged each other's presence, at least Tom did.

He was able to see Jess again. She was delighted to see him without fresh injuries.

As Tom sat there with her he tried to rationalise how all this had happened. Yet try as he might he couldn't find a logical path from the killing of Liam Burgess to him being in prison, about to stand trial for two other killings and an attempted murder of a third.

As he spoke he took something from his pocket. He placed it on the table in front of him. It was a tobacco pouch. Tom took a paper from the pouch and laid it on the table. He then began to make a cigarette.

Jess's eyes widened. "You've started again? Can't say I'm surprised. Probably got little else to do with your time in here."

Tom raised his gaze towards her from what he was doing, he gave her a pitiful look. Almost an apologetic look.

"I guess the hypnosis only works for so long between sessions, I guess I'm a little overdue," he said, chuckling as he did.

"I've had a couple of chats with my legal team," Tom began, "they've reviewed everything that's happened so far, and what they've been allowed to see of the prosecution's case. They've said I've got a fighting chance, it's by no means cut and dried, but I should equally prepare myself for a rough ride. I've tried to tell them that I didn't do what I'm accused of, they've said they believe me, but that there's evidence to the contrary. I've been having a couple of sessions a month with shrinks who feel they've got an understanding of what's going on; it's some sleep-walking type paranoia, that I'm not of sound mind when I'm doing all this. They're getting some psych experts in to testify."

He realised he must look as equally as confused as Jess did staring back at him, trying to make sense of how they've ended up having a

196

conversation across a table in the prison visitor's centre.

Jess then raised a sympathetic smile. She began to extend a hand across the table towards where Tom's hand was moulding tobacco within the paper. She then recalled the rules and withdrew it partially. She looked over at a guard who was now paying particular attention to them.

After a moment, her gaze left the watchful guard and it panned across the room.

Their last visit had been afforded the luxury of them being the only visit in the room at that time. This time the visitors centre was busy, several other prisoners were also enjoying a visit. Some were being visited by a single person, whilst a couple of the others had entire families including children visiting them.

This is no place for children she thought, shaking her head as she did, feeling it was such a minor gesture that no one would notice.

"What's up?" Tom asked.

"Oh, it's nothing," she said, "I was just thinking that this was no place for children, that's all."

Tom scanned the room himself, he saw the children at the tables. He had to agree with Jess on some level, but after the time he had spent in prison, he could understand the joy that such a gesture would afford the prisoner.

"Sometimes it's the only pleasure in this place," he said, "having something to look forward to is what makes this place bearable."

"This'll be our last visit here," Tom continued, "I'm being transferred down south again over the weekend so I'm local come Monday morning."

The imminence of the trial upset Jess and she started to well up in front of Tom.

Her hand was still there on the table in front of him. Without even checking to see if any of the guards were looking Tom extended his hand out and placed it on top of hers. Their thumbs instinctively intertwined. Jess looked at him, Tom looked back trying to reassure her that everything would be all right. She smiled.

Their hands held across the table until a guard happened to see them.

"TABLE SIX – NO CONTACT!" a voice bellowed from the side of the room.

Normally, Tom would've reacted instantly and retracted his hand on command. But neither of them reacted in any way.

"TABLE SIX, I SAID NO CONTACT!" came the order, more assertive than before.

Still, there was no reaction from Tom, he felt Jess try to pull her hand from beneath his, but Tom defiantly held her hand in position.

Jess looked around the room in panic.

She could see several guards approaching their table from different directions. She tried desperately to reclaim her hand from Tom. Although she desired the contact from him, she didn't want this.

She looked at Tom's face and saw an expression she had never seen from him before. It scared her.

As the three guards reached their table, Tom released the pressure that pinned Jess's hand to it. He raised his hands to either side of his head as if someone had pointed a gun at him and said 'hands up'. One guard was now standing directly behind him, the other two flanked him.

Tom stood up in a blur, so fast that it put the guards on the defensive. They all took a step back and lowered their stance preparing for a physical confrontation.

Tom turned to face the guard that had addressed him. Whatever he was thinking about to antagonise the guards had been lost in the realisation that Jess was sitting across from him and that she would undoubtedly get caught up in any mêlée.

"You were warned about the contact, Draven," said the guard who had shouted across the room at him.

"I warned you twice," he continued, holding up the middle and forefingers of his right hand as if he felt further emphasis was required.

He then felt further dominance was needed as Tom stood defiantly in front of him. He prodded Tom in the middle of his chest with the two fingers.

"When I tell you to do something, Draven," the guard paused, "you do it, understand?"

Tom suddenly had a feeling of déjà vu. This confrontation had an eerie familiarity to it, more than a dream, more than an account given by a fellow inmate. Once again, a confused look fell across Tom's face.

Time slowed for him as he looked down at the fingers prodding his chest. His instinct was to grab these fingers and inflict pain. This confused him further; why would he feel the desire to react in this way?

As he looked down he could see his left hand autonomously raising itself up towards the outstretched fingers of the guard.

Tom felt like an audience member to his own pantomime. He wasn't able to interact in any way, or was he?

So far no one had seen his physical defiance beyond standing up. Although the guards had taken a step backwards they were all still standing too close to see what his hands were doing below waist height.

In a moment of clarity, Tom thought better of it. He wanted the fight, and perhaps under different circumstances he would've provoked the situation further, but not with Jess sitting less than a metre away.

In a swift moment, Tom spun his torso to his right to squarely face Jess again. In doing so he knocked the guard's outstretched arm with such force to spin him off balance.

Tom looked at Jess with apparent disregard of the act of defiance he had just demonstrated in a room full of guards, prisoners and their families.

"I'll see you next week," he said to Jess.

She smiled, her hand still extended to the middle of the table. Realising this, she cautiously withdrew it and buried it beneath the table.

"You're done," the guard said. The visit session had several minutes left, but given Tom's display, his would be abruptly cut short.

The other two guards then turned Tom so that he was facing his exit and started ushering him towards it.

Beyond the door was a hallway, which required Tom and the guards to turn right. In turning right, Tom was able to glance back into the room and give Jess a brief reassuring smile before disappearing out of sight.

Once out of sight, the remaining guard explained the situation to Jess and suggested to her that it was also her time to leave.

Then, in the time it took to make this suggestion, an alarm sounded from beyond the visitor's centre.

From where Jess was standing she couldn't see any commotion. Yet through the doorway that Tom had just passed through she could see guards rushing in the direction that Tom had gone only seconds earlier.

She brought her hands up in front of her face unable to believe what was happening. "Oh my God, Tom."

DAY 126

"All rise," the court usher cried.

The judge entered the courtroom to see the jury on their feet as well as Tom, who stood dressed in civilian clothes beside his robed and wigged barrister, and across from them was the legal team for the Crown.

"Please be seated," came the order, the court was now in session.

Due to the nature of the trial and the status of the defendant the public gallery had been closed off to the general public. The only occupants today were representatives of the media. Newspaper reporters and TV journalists could be seen as well as the occasional artists making renderings of the proceedings as this courtroom was not fitted with any broadcasting cameras.

In the time Tom had been in prison awaiting trial a considerable amount of public interest had generated around the case. However, a court ruling had made any publication or broadcast of Tom's name or image illegal. It was this ruling that spared Tom significantly more grief in prison than what he actually had to endure.

The twelve members of the jury had been selected during the time that Tom had been in prison. Again, given Tom's status in the community, the selection process was more stringent than usual. The questioning as part of the selection process of prospective jurors included delving into their respective backgrounds as well as asking of any prejudices they may have against the police as a whole.

Beyond the teams of the prosecution and defence, the other court officials included the clerks, a stenographer and a translator.

Tom was now becoming increasingly aware of why the translator was there. He had several meetings with the defence team during his incarceration, however they omitted their strategy until the final meeting, included in which was their plan for tackling the likelihood of various elements of the prosecution's case.

Their strategy centred around expert witnesses explaining to the court that Tom was in fact innocent of the charges against him, as opposed to discrediting witnesses or the physical evidence before them.

But before any of that could take place the prosecution had to prove the case against him. The prosecution stood first to give the court their opening speech.

"Ladies and gentlemen of the jury, the Crown thanks you for your service, I thank you for your service, and I will also thank you in advance for your patience, because this trial will try you too. This trial is of a police officer, a man who has taken an oath to protect the people of this country against the very thing he is on trial for. A man who was sworn into the office of constable as a trusted member of our community. He stands before you today charged with two gruesome and heinous murders and the attempted murder of another, who only by sheer luck avoided becoming his third victim. You will hear about his victims through the course of this trial, but I will introduce them to you now: Pauline Barnes, a forty-seven-year-old mother of two, a home carer for the terminally ill. You will hear how she was stabbed in the back of the head as she sat in her car in a multi-storey car park after having finished her shopping."

The barrister paused long enough to allow the jury's reaction to sink in. He observed a look of disgust as some of the members glanced across the courtroom to where Tom sat, appearing to have already rendered their verdict.

Tom, who was well practiced in attending court, having given testimony on countless occasions, was doing his best to ignore the stares and glances.

Having received the reaction he sought, the barrister continued.

"You will also hear about Ronald Campbell, a sixty-seven-year retiree who lived only to serve the community in which he lived. Ronald had retired at an early age due to ill-health yet continued to serve his community by being a lollipop man at his local primary school. He was also a scout leader for his local pack as well as participating in numerous charity fundraising efforts to benefit those less fortunate than him."

Again, the prosecution barrister paused long enough to allow the splendour of Campbell's lifetime of community giving to sink in.

"You will also hear heart-wrenching testimony from the only person to escape with their life. Leanne Young will stand before you and have you witness her ordeal as she relives it for you. I will ask on behalf of Pauline Barnes and Ronald Campbell that you see that justice is served here, I have no doubt that Leanne will ask you for herself. Thank you."

The barrister retook his seat, adjusted it under the table and scribbled some quick notes to himself.

Tom's barrister, the legal representation for the defence, then stood. He adjusted his gown and turned to face the jury as his counterpart had just done.

"Ladies and gentleman, good morning. What my learned colleague has told you today is true; Pauline Barnes and Ronald Campbell paid with their lives for what happened on those awful dates, and Leanne Young barely escaped with her life, and for that we are all grateful. You will hear some damning testimony from expert witnesses, including police officers and forensic specialists, and what I have no doubt will be a heart-wrenching testimony from Ms Young herself. But what I will say to you now is that the man sat across from you" — he paused and turned and lifted his hand in a gesture towards where Tom sat — "this man, Thomas Draven, did not commit the crimes for which he is charged and for which you will hear about during this trial. Now I am not saying that they didn't die by his hand, but this man DID – NOT – KILL anyone."

The defence pondered on this point long enough for the words he used to sink in and what he had actually said to be absorbed. This reaction was realised when a perplexed look fell across the jury.

Realising his work was done he thanked the jury and again took his seat.

The prosecution then began their case. As Tom was charged with three separate offences each had to be proven separately and independently of each other so that the jury could decide each charge on its own merits, and not be compelled to decide that if Tom was guilty of one that he must be guilty of them all and vice versa.

The prosecution had chosen to try to prove each case in a reverse chronological order. The defence was aware of this strategy, as was Tom. When discussed between Tom and the defence team it appeared illogical; typically, cases would normally be presented in the order they were committed, which would make Young's case the last one to be heard. Given that she was the only surviving witness, this would also make her testimony the last thing the jury heard, which would be a powerful way for the prosecution to close their argument. The only reason the defence could think of was that this would allow Leanne

Young to give her testimony as early on in the trial as possible thus sparing her any prolonged anguish.

The first witness to be called to the stand to prove the case in the attempted murder of Leanne Young was the police constable who arrested Tom at his home address some four months ago.

He gave evidence about Tom's arrest and the items that were seized at the time of his arrest and the subsequent search of his home address.

The prosecutor kept repeating, "I will make future reference to this," and, "future reference to that."

The prosecutor ended his examination of this witness by making a request to recall him as necessary, which was acknowledged by the court.

Tom's barrister leant across to address him. When interrupted by the judge asking if he wished to ask this witness any questions, he declined. The officer was dismissed.

The next witness to take the stand was a scientific support officer from the police force investigating the attempted murder of Leanne Young.

After being sworn in, introducing herself and giving her credentials she was asked by the prosecutor to explain to the court the physical evidence that linked the defendant to the victim and the crime scene.

She began by explaining how the samples were taken from the victim. In this case by having scrapings taken from beneath each fingernail, and then the nails themselves were clipped and seized as evidence.

The victim's clothing was also seized. This was done for two reasons: first of all, in case there was any forensic transfer between the parties involved, and secondly, it illustrated what the victim was wearing at the time of the incident, and the condition the clothing ended up in as a result of the attack.

For this to be shown to the court a TV monitor had been brought in, and the witness was giving commentary to a slide show presentation.

The images shown to the court included the area of wasteland where the attack was alleged to have taken place. It started with wide angle shots which narrowed and became more focused on the actual crime scene itself.

The witness explained that although the shots shown were taken during daylight the actual attack took place at night, and with no lighting in the area, it would've taken place in moonlight only.

The witness then proceeded to describe the methods by which DNA is extracted and exposed for comparison, and with this came several images illustrating the procedure.

The final image showed the DNA sequence retrieved from samples taken from the victim compared against a sequence stated to be that of Tom Draven.

Once the witness had finished the prosecutor thanked her for her testimony and took his seat.

The defence barrister rose. He didn't circle around the table to approach the witness box to address the witness. He spoke from where he stood.

"Please could you tell the court how you came about a sample of the defendant's DNA?"

As the witness began to answer he had already retaken his seat. He already knew the answer, he just felt the court needed to hear it too.

"The defendant's sample was obtained when he first joined the police force," the witness replied.

"So how old is this sample?" he then asked.

This was an answer the witness didn't have. "From when he first joined the police," she repeated.

"And did you have to obtain a court warrant to access this historic sample?"

"No, sir, all officers enter into an understanding for their profiles, both DNA and fingerprints to be kept and used for comparative and elimination purposes."

Content with the answers he had received he said, "I have no further questions for this witness."

After the forensic officer was dismissed, court was adjourned for the day.

DAY 127

The next day started the same as the first with the judge being the last to enter the courtroom.

The only change was that the translator was now sitting between the defendant and his barrister.

There was only one witness on the docket for today, the victim herself, Leanne Young.

It was stated that Leanne couldn't give testimony from within the courtroom itself, so her evidence would be given by a live CCTV video link from another room within the court building. It was a live interactive feed that would allow her to hear what the court had to ask as well as the court being able to hear her responses.

As Young was a witness for the prosecution it was the prosecutor who addressed her first. After the introductions and an explanation as to why the video link was necessary, the prosecutor asked Young to give her account of what had happened.

"It was late in the evening, I was working. It started to rain so I was gonna call it a day and go home. I was getting my stuff together when a guy comes up to me and asks me if I'm still working. I says yes, coz I needs the money. I say where? coz they usually have a car and he didn't. He points behind the fence where we were and says *there*, so we go through the fence and he leads me for a bit before stopping. I remember looking back and barely being able to see the street lights. It was then he hit me on the head. I fell down and he tried to strangle me." Young paused to compose herself. "He's on top of me, strangling me, then somehow, I managed to kick him off me and make a run for it. I ran back to the street screaming. A car stopped and took me to hospital."

"Thank you for your testimony, Miss Young, I know that couldn't have been easy for you. I do have a few questions for you now if you're happy to continue?" the prosecutor asked.

On the TV screen, Young could be seen to nod as she was wiping her eyes with a tissue.

"Do you recall how you fought off your attacker?"

"Yes, I do," Young replied, "after he pushed me to the ground he straddled me. He had one of my arms pinned under him, and the other he held

214

down with his hand. I couldn't see very well because of the light but it looks like he was reaching into his pocket for something."

"Do you know what he was reaching for, did you see it?"

"No, I didn't," Young replied, "but then he started talking to me."

"What did he say?"

"He sounded different, but he said 'you have one chance to confess, confess now and I'll spare you'," Young answered.

"You say he sounded *different,* different how exactly?"

"When he spoke to me in the street he spoke with an accent, very few words, but this was a different voice with no accent."

"And then what happened?"

"I felt his hold on me loosen, I managed to get my arm free from beneath him. I started to struggle, and I think he lost his balance coz he let go of my other arm. He then toppled backwards, and I kicked him. He fell to the ground and I started to get myself up, saw he wasn't moving, I dunno he must've hit his head or something. So, I just ran back to the street."

"Miss Young, yesterday the forensic expert stated that samples were collected from you and that DNA evidence was under your fingernails, are you able to say how that got there?"

"Dunno for sure, when he was strangling me, I did grab his wrists to pull them off me, could've happened then, I s'pose."

The prosecutor then went back to his bench and retrieved something from his briefcase. Whatever it was it was small, small enough to be entirely concealed within one hand. He walked back and stood in front of the TV screen which had a camera on top and microphones below, as much as standing in front of Leanne Young herself.

"Miss Young," he began, "I would like to ask you to close your eyes. I am then going to have something said to you, and I want you to tell me if you recognise the voice you hear, is that okay?"

Young nodded in agreement. She took a deep breath in frightful anticipation of what was about to happen. She closed her eyes.

With his back to the courtroom and jury, and with only the judge being able to see what he was doing, the prosecutor held in front of him the item he had just taken from his briefcase. But even the judge couldn't make out what it was yet.

The court was silent.

The prosecutor could see that Young was obviously frightened, not knowing what was coming. He didn't want to prolong the agony. He activated the item held in his hand.

A voice spoke breaking the silence, 'you have one chance to live, confess now and I'll spare your life, tell me everything you want to confess, now'.

Young tensed up in terror, squeezing her eyes closed even further. From the where the prosecutor stood he could see more of Young than anyone in the courtroom. He could see her fingers turn white as she grasped the fabric of her trousers as she sat with her hands on her lap on a chair in the centre of the broadcast.

"Miss Young," he said in a calm voice, "you can open your eyes now, thank you. Do you recognise the voice you've just heard?"

Young opened her eyes, they were full of tears, a couple escaped down her face as she set her gaze on the prosecutor.

"Did you recognise the voice you just heard?" He paused long enough for her to voice a reply. "Was this the same voice you heard whilst you were being attacked?"

"Yes," she said softly, still traumatised at having to relive that aspect of her ordeal.

The prosecutor then held aloft a small digital voice dictation machine. He pressed the play button again and allowed the court to hear the voice on it for a second time. It was not a spoken human voice, it was a synthesised digital male voice, *you have one chance to live, confess now and I'll spare your life.* This time the chilling ultimatum echoed around the courtroom. Then the deathly quiet returned.

"Thank you, Miss Young, I have no more questions. I would like to enter this as prosecution exhibit *papa-bravo-zero-one.*"

The judge then addressed Leanne Young via the video link, "Are you okay to continue, Miss Young, or would you like a short recess?"

"I'm okay," she replied.

The judge then acknowledged to the defence that they may now start their cross-examination of the witness.

There was a delay in response as the defence realised why they had decided to prove the cases in the order they did; why they had chosen to have Leanne Young testify so early in the trial. The prosecution had already proven beyond all reasonable doubt that the defendant's DNA was found on the victim. That put him in direct physical contact with her.

Now, the introduction of this exhibit a more substantial link to the other offences for which they had no DNA evidence had not been established. That is why the dictating machine was entered into court evidence as exhibit *papa-bravo one*. This exhibit related to the Barnes case. *Papa-bravo* is the phonetic alphabet for P-B referring to, in this instance, Pauline Barnes. This exhibit related to the Pauline Barnes murder. This exhibit now created a link between the Young case and the Barnes case, and with the defendant forensically linked to the Young case, it would no doubt give further credence to the jury with regards to the Barnes case and possibly the Campbell case too.

Putting Young on the stand so soon had absolutely nothing to do with having her testify early in order to minimise her agony.

The defence barrister did his best to hide his frustration. He looked to his left, the translator sat dormant having received no instruction to speak, and beyond him, the defendant sat still, possibly unaware of what had just transpired.

"Are you ready, sir?" the judge asked.

The defence barrister nodded and stood, he adjusted his robes and circled the bench to stand square to the camera for the video link.

"Miss Young, you've given a truly horrendous account of what happened that night. First of all, I'd like to establish why you were there. Why were you there at that time of night, on your own, in the middle of a run-down, derelict industrial estate?"

"I was working," came her reply.

"I know, you said you were working in your account, but can you be specific please, for the benefit of the court."

"I'm a tom," Young replied.

"Please can you clarify that slang term into something the court may understand?"

"A prostitute," she said softly.

The defence felt it unnecessary to ask her to repeat it any louder. He heard her, he was sure the court heard her too.

The term *tom,* referring to a prostitute is rhyming slang, some claiming it derives from *Thomas More* resulting as *whore.*

"Okay, now we know why you were there. And equally, we all know the risks that those in this profession can put themselves under," he said.

A hush fell, and the defence could feel the cold stare of the judge on him. There was a line drawn when it came to the treatment of vulnerable witnesses, and he felt he was close to it, but as nothing had been said he had yet to cross it.

"You say that you were about to go home because it had been a slow night for you, had you had any business that evening?"

"Yeah, that's right."

"And typically, how much business do you get, shall we say on an average week?" the defence barrister asked.

"Depends."

"Depends on what?" He paused. "Miss Young, from what I understand your client base has greatly dwindled in recent months. Would you say that to be an accurate statement?"

Young could be seen to nod on the TV screen.

"And why is that, do you think?" he asked.

She shook her head. "Dunno."

"I believe I do." He paused. "Is it true that you are HIV positive, Miss Young?"

The defence was waiting for an interruption or an objection from the judge or prosecution that never came.

"Is it true that in the time since your diagnosis you've been unable to sustain a regular income, that you now advertise to not require contraception in order to drum up more business?"

Young did not respond.

"Is it true that you're bitter at having contracted this disease, and that you've stated to people that, oh how was it phrased..." He paused to scan-read a document to find the highlighted passage. "...Ah, here it is, you've stated that you're *gonna make others suffer as I am?* Is this true, are you intentionally going out of your way to infect people, and that's the real reason why you no longer use contraception?"

Still silence.

"Miss Young, do the names Angus Fletcher and Douglas Cable mean anything to you?" He paused long enough to expect a response. When none came he continued, "Is it true that you are under investigation for intentionally and recklessly infecting these two men with this disease? And if they're infected and willing to come forward, then how many more are there who are as yet unaware?"

"That's enough!" The judge's interruption seemed to bring an overwhelming sigh of relief from all those present.

"I'm sorry, My Lord," apologised the defence.

"Lastly, Miss Young, there hasn't been a single reported attack on a prostitute in this, or the surrounding areas, for quite some time. Do you feel you were targeted because of your intention to spread this disease?"

"That's enough, the jury will disregard that last remark," the judge instructed.

"I have nothing further, My Lord." And he retook his seat. As he sat he could hear the translator putting the last of the account to the defendant who was smiling.

Leanne Young was dismissed as a witness. Via the CCTV link, she could be seen to be consoled by someone who had entered the frame.

What followed was a summarisation of the facts of the Young case to the jury for them to deliberate upon. There was no doubt that the item the judge had ordered them to disregard would hang strongly in their minds. This was specifically why it was the last thing the defence mentioned before closing.

The defence couldn't dispute the forensic evidence. What they had to do was to suggest a *why* to go with the *who,* the *where,* the *when* and the *how* that they already had.

They hadn't gained anything, and they hadn't lost anything over Young's testimony. Their day was still to come.

DAY 128

With the Young case argued it was time to move on to laying the evidence in the case of Ronald Campbell. Unlike the Young case, there were no witnesses to the actual murder, so this would be a case proven based on physical evidence.

The prosecution's case opened by explaining how Campbell's body was found, lying in his bed at home. The physical signs of injury to the body were illustrated on a TV monitor by means of photographs and body mapped diagrams. The pathological evidence then explained how these injuries led to Campbell's death.

Once again, the defence did not feel the need to question the account or conclusions offered by the prosecution as to how Campbell died.

Following the physical evidence, the prosecution called to the stand the first police officer who arrived on the scene at Campbell's home address.

He was asked questions about how he found the address, were there any signs of a break-in, were there any signs of a disturbance within the property? The officer stated that aside from the dead body in the bed the property was all in order, and that it was found locked and secure prior to him forcing entry.

Next to take the stand was Detective Sergeant Eddie Poulton.

After taking the affirmation, the prosecution began their examination of the witness. "Please can you explain your findings after you attended Campbell's home address?"

"The call came to police from the deceased's GP after a missed appointment. Following that, uniformed officers attended the address, and when they failed to get an answer they forced entry. Once inside, they found the body of Mister Campbell. An ambulance was immediately called, and CID were notified. It was then that I attended."

"And why was the defendant there?" the prosecution asked.

"As a professional courtesy between neighbouring forces, I called DC Carl Wainwright. I knew he was investigating a murder, so I wanted his take on this scene in case there were any similarities."

"Then what happened?"

"Wainwright attended the location with the defendant who is his supervisor. They were signed into the log and were allowed into the scene."

There was a pause in Poulton's account as the prosecutor held up the scene log that recorded Draven and Wainwright's attendance at Campbell's home address. "Please go on, detective."

"They then entered Campbell's house with me, I showed them both the deceased and gave them both a briefing as to what we knew to that point. I then gave them free rein of the house, they were able to go anywhere unescorted."

"How long were they at the location, detective?"

"Without referring to the scene log, I would only be able to guess, I'd say maybe twenty minutes," Poulton replied.

"The log states that the defendant and DS Wainwright were at the scene between ten-eighteen and ten-thirty-nine, that's twenty-one minutes."

"Did the defendant have gloves on whenever you saw him at the scene?" the prosecutor asked.

"Yes," Poulton replied.

The prosecutor then returned to his desk and was handed a small evidence bag and a photograph by his colleague. He then walked back towards the witness box and handed the photograph to Poulton.

"Please can you describe what this item is?"

"This is a Lego key ring comprising of a policeman figure that was photographed on the corner shelves in Campbell's living room," Poulton replied.

The prosecutor then approached the jury and showed them photographic images of the key ring figure standing on a shelf in Campbell's living room. The images started as an overall of the living room, before focusing in on the shelves, then the single shelf, then the figure itself.

The prosecutor then returned to his bench, placed the photographs back down and was then handed a report by his colleague. He then handed the report to Poulton and asked him to read the highlighted passage.

"The exhibit romeo-charlie zero-seven was examined and a sample was extracted. The sample matches a profile held in the name of the defendant."

The prosecutor then went on to explain that the report made by the scenes of crime officer, who had attended the location and taken the photographs seen in the report, had confirmed that they were date/time stamped to show the exhibit in question was present at the location prior to the defendant being booked into the scene log.

The prosecutor then again returned to his bench to be handed yet another evidence bag and another photograph. He returned to stand in front of DS Poulton.

"Please can you explain to the court what this item, marked as court exhibit romeo-charlie-one-four is, and where it was found?"

"Court exhibit romeo-charlie-one-four is described as being a digital recording machine, and it was found on the bedside table of the deceased's bedroom."

"And have you had a chance to listen to any recordings on this device?" the prosecutor asked.

"Yes, I have, there are two audio files, made by two different male voices," Poulton replied.

"If it pleases the court, My Lord, I would like to now play the two audio files that have been duplicated from this device."

The judge nodded his agreement. With that, the prosecutor's assistant activated a remote which played the first audio recorded.

"You have one chance to live, confess now and I'll spare your life, tell me everything you want to confess, now."

The remote control was again activated to pause the playback.

The prosecutor looked over at the jury, they had just heard the exact same monotonous tone spoken from a device found at the home of Ronald Campbell that was heard the previous day to send chills down the spine of Leanne Young.

"I will now play you the second recording," the prosecutor continued and again signalled to his colleague.

A whispered heavily accented voice could be heard to say, "S*tate you name*," before another voice started talking.

"...ease don't kill me [grunt], my name is Ronald Campbell, for years now I have been abusing young boys in my care, [sniff], I have convictions in Australia, [sniff] but I came back to England to carry on here, [grunt of pain], I applied for a role as a scout leader so I could be trusted to be alone with young boys, [grunt of pain], on camp I would encourage the boys to share my tent, and to tell me stories. Then I would tell them stories to scare them, so they would ask to sleep in my tent overnight, I would then touch

them whilst they slept, [uncontrollable sobbing], I'm sorry for what I've done, I can't help myself [pause], I've done what you've asked, you said you'd let me g..."

The recording ended, and the prosecutor's colleague stopped the playback.

A stunned silence fell over the courtroom having just listened to the last words of a dead man, where little doubt remained that the man was killed immediately after having made a confession in a desperate attempt to spare his life.

The judge broke the silence by calling a break for lunch. That concluded the evidence that Poulton was required to give for the prosecution. After lunch would come the defence barrister's turn to address the witness.

The prosecutor looked over at the defendant who was sitting next to his barrister. Today there sat only the two of them, today the translator was not needed. He sat elsewhere in the courtroom should he be required. The defendant understood everything that was just said and seemed to be as shocked by the recording as anyone else in the courtroom.

When the trial resumed, the judge indicated to the defence to continue and begin their cross-examination of Poulton.

The defence barrister was sitting at the bench discussing matters with the defendant when the judge addressed him.

The conversation between them ended with the defendant nodding as the barrister rose to his feet. He then approached where DS Poulton sat in the witness box. After they exchanged pleasantries with each other the cross-examination began.

"DS Poulton, I understand from the scene log that you were at the location prior to the defendant's arrival, and also there long after his departure, is this correct?"

"Yes."

"And was the defendant in your presence the entire time?"

"No, he wasn't, after showing him around and showing him the body of the deceased, he and DC Wainwright were allowed to examine the scene as they saw fit," Poulton replied.

"Did they feed anything back to you after they had finished at the scene, and did they report to you any similarities between their investigation and your own?"

"No, they did not."

"And can you confirm that the recording device was seized on the same day as all the other exhibits?"

There was a pause before Poulton responded, "No, it wasn't, that exhibit was seized several days after the rest."

"Several days you say," said the defence. "According to the case records, this exhibit was not seized for a couple of weeks after the scene had been closed. After the property had been released back to Mister Campbell's family, and it was only their scrutinisation of this item that brought it to your attention in the first place, is that right Detective Sergeant Poulton?"

"Yes, that is correct, the family found the item on the floor behind the bedside table," Poulton admitted.

"Why wasn't this item found by your officers when they attended the scene?" the prosecution asked.

"I can't answer that," Poulton answered, looking embarrassed.

"So, what you're essentially saying is that there is nothing to connect that exhibit to the case? You only have a statement from a member of Mister Campbell's family to place this item at the scene and to verify that the second voice heard is that of Ronald Campbell."

"Yes, that is correct," Poulton said looking like a scolded schoolchild.

"So, would you say that this calls into question any other evidence you have linking the defendant to that scene?" the defence said rhetorically, yet still pausing as if to expect a reply. "I have no more questions, My Lord."

"The witness is dismissed," the judge said.

That concluded the trial for the day.

The defence team remained to discuss the day's proceedings with their client.

"Tom, today certainly hasn't done us any harm. There's nothing to link you to the location, and the recording doesn't prove anything. There's enough delay there for the jury to draw their own conclusions, and more importantly, raise sufficient doubt."

He looked across at Tom, who looked distraught. It wasn't, however, because he was on trial, but because he was as shocked at hearing a condemned man's confession and pleas for mercy as anyone else in the room. He had seen their reactions, which no doubt mirrored his own.

"I haven't been able to determine whether or not that recording came to be before or after Young's account was first given to the police. It's not date-stamped and there's nothing to even prove it to be Campbell's voice other than a family member's say-so. I fully expect tomorrow to go the same way." The barrister paused. "Try not to worry, get yourself a good night's sleep and I'll see you in the morning, okay?"

Tom was not so sure but nodded along to bring the conversation to an end.

DAY 129

Like the previous day, the laying of evidence in the case of Pauline Barnes began with the prosecutor giving an overview of the case.

He began by describing the location of the killing, that being an upper floor of a multi-storey car park. How Barnes was killed, by a single puncture wound to the base of the skull, and how she was discovered, by a motorist who had parked in a nearby bay and seen someone slumped at the wheel and approached their vehicle. They found it to be locked, and saw the victim with her head forward, but there was enough light to see blood and matted hair. They then called the police.

The prosecutor then went on to describe what the police found when they attended the scene. Barnes' car, a grey Audi A1, was indeed found locked and secured, the keys were in the ignition. There were no signs of a robbery, and no signs of a struggle. The overview also included that a single button from an item of clothing was located at the scene.

The contents of the car, all personal items on Barnes and in her shopping, had been documented. The prosecutor paid particular attention to the list of items in her handbag. He read out the contents, "One purse, one lipstick, compact mirror, mobile phone, packet of tissues, chewing gum, Dictaphone, foundation, mascara, hair clips, three pens, sewing kit, miscellaneous receipts, sunglasses, tampons, hand cream, medication, and sweeteners."

He didn't ponder on any specific item, it was as if he was just putting it out there to be referred to later on.

The forensic expert then gave testimony. This testimony explained that Barnes was found in her car and was declared dead at the scene, what position her body was found in, and the physical trauma found to her body which was documented at the scene as well as the subsequent autopsy. A slide show of images illustrated the points being made.

This was then elaborated on by means of the coroner's report. It stated that the cause of death came as the result of a single puncture wound into the cerebellum at the base of the skull. The report then went on to describe the location and function of the cerebellum as well as the kinesiology of such an injury.

Barnes was also described as having diagonal bruising across her torso. This was explained as being consistent with the seatbelt being tightened across her body. Again, images gave further illustration. It was further explained that the bruising most likely occurred after Barnes had sat in her car, and she had put the keys in the ignition, she then put on her seatbelt probably before starting the engine. It was then that she was attacked from behind. The seatbelt being pulled tight by her attacker and causing pressure across her chest.

The forensic expert was then asked to give testimony of an item seized next to the vehicle following the discovery of Barnes' body.

The item was described simply as a *brown button* and was marked as court exhibit papa-bravo zero-eight. It was then explained that this button was identical to the buttons on a jacket that was seized from the home address of the defendant. Photographic images were shown to the court of the button and the jacket that had been seized. At the same time, the prosecutor held aloft the actual items in police evidence bags and paraded them before the jury.

After the prosecution had finished with their witness the court had a short recess, after which it was the defence's opportunity to perform a cross-examination.

"Please can you state again where exactly this button was located?" the defence asked.

"The button was found, photographed and seized from the ground adjacent to the nearside rear door of the victim's vehicle."

"And was the coat you seized from the home address of the defendant in fact missing a button?"

"No, sir," came the reply.

"And did the jacket seized from the home of the defendant look like it had ever had a button replaced?"

Again, the reply was negative.

"So, this could just be an unfortunate coincidence then?" the defence barrister concluded.

There was a pause, no reply was forthcoming. The judge dismissed the witness.

oOo

After the break for lunch, the prosecutor again stood before the court.

"This morning you may recall I listed the contents of the victim's handbag. Amongst them was an item that has been determined not to belong to the victim, it has since been analysed and this item will not appear alien to you." He paused. "Left in her handbag by her killer are the last words she would ever say."

Having built the suspense he felt necessary, he returned to his bench to be handed an evidence bag and photograph. The evidence bag contained the now familiar digital voice recorder that had already been seen by the court twice this week. This time upon signalling to his colleague the court would hear the last words of Pauline Barnes.

"...arnes, I know I've done wrong, I've hurt people, I've done it for greed, all I wanted was a better life, [pause], I've worked hard with nothing to show for it. They were dying anyway, they didn't need what they had, they could afford it. I needed it more than they did. I deserved it more than their families who never visited. I was the one who changed them, fed them, cleared up their shit, and for what? [pause] A couple of them then put me in their wills, so yeah, I helped them on their way, *they went peacefully. [pause] I've done what you've asked, now will y…"*

The recording ended. As before, the court was left in silence.

The prosecutor broke the silence. "We've had testimony from the family of Pauline Barnes confirming that this is her voice on the recording."

Once again Tom sat beside his barrister, a look of stunned sadness on his face.

He had a vague recollection of the confessions he'd heard, but to him, they were never anything more than a dream.

There was nothing for the defence to cross-examine on this evidence as this digital recorder had been seized into evidence at the time police had attended the initial scene. It was understood that it wasn't scrutinised until sometime after the murder after taken place, and only after similarities between this case and the others became apparent. But the chain of evidence had been maintained, unlike that in the Campbell investigation.

With this evidence heard, the prosecution confirmed that they had stated their case. The judge then adjourned the court until the next day when the defence would begin their case.

DAY 130

The defence's case did not necessarily have to prove that the defendant was innocent, all they had to do was to raise reasonable doubt in the mind of the jury who would then have no choice but to acquit.

This could be done by means of offering alternative plausible explanations for how or why things have taken place, or by undermining the evidence or testimony that has been offered by the prosecution.

The defence barrister began by giving an overview of points made during the prosecution's case and addressed them individually.

"Ladies and gentlemen of the jury, firstly please let me remind you that the defendant is on trial for the deaths of two people and the attempted murder of a third. It is your role to find him guilty beyond any reasonable doubt. You are not governed to find him guilty of all or none, but it is your responsibility to reach verdicts on each case individually. Finding the defendant guilty of one case should not sway you to find him guilty of any other."

The first witness was then sworn in, and after making his introduction and stating his area of speciality the defence barrister began his questioning.

"Since Tom Draven, the man sat across the courtroom from us, was charged with two murders and the attempted murder of a third, he has spent his time in prison awaiting this trial, and during this time you have met with him on many occasions, is this correct?"

"Yes *and* no," the expert, a Professor White, replied.

This reply caused confusion to be seen on every face in the courtroom, including the judge and members of the jury. In fact, everyone except for the defence team.

"And why do you say that?" the barrister enquired.

"Yes, I met with Tom Draven on many occasions during the time he was in prison, and no, that is not Tom Draven sat across the courtroom from me today."

This response caused even more confusion to air about the room.

With that, he looked across at the defence's bench where the defendant sat with a man who had previously been sitting between him and his legal representative.

"Allow me to explain," the expert requested.

"Please do," said the barrister, gesturing as if the room was his to address.

"Thank you. Tom Draven suffers from a rare, but not unique Dissociative Personality *or* Identity Disorder," he paused to allow the information he had just imparted to be absorbed by the audience. He continued, "This is known as having a disjointed, or more commonly referred to as a split personality. In Tom's case, his alternate personality is a male known as Tomasz, he is Polish, or believes himself to be Polish. Tom cannot speak or understand a word of Polish, yet Tomasz is fluent, conversely having only very basic English. And the reason for my initial response is because it is Tomasz that sits before us today, the man sat next to him is his translator."

The expert paused, and the eyes of the court settled on Tomasz who appeared to be in conference with the man sat beside him, when in reality Tomasz was receiving a translation of the proceedings.

When Tomasz heard his name mentioned he took this as being his introduction to the court and looked around with a slight smile as if to acknowledge his name being said to the court for the very first time.

The barrister then entered into the questions he and the expert had arranged and rehearsed.

"Has Tom always experienced this?"

"I don't believe so," replied the professor, "I believe the potential for this has always been with Tom, but in my opinion the hypnosis he underwent to assist him to stop smoking acted as a catalyst."

"So what effect did this have on Tom?"

"Well, hypnosis taps into the sub-consciousness, in the case of overcoming a phobia or habit it places a subliminal suggestion or aversion in the subject's psyche. However, with inexperience or error on the part of the hypnotherapist, something else can be suggested. In Tom's case, I feel a doorway was inadvertently created and left open within his subconscious, and on the other side of that doorway a manifestation was created, and that manifestation created its own personality and identity, who we now know to be Tomasz Dravidas."

"So, who is Tomasz Dravidas?" the barrister asked.

"He is no one, he was never born, essentially he doesn't exist. He is an amalgamation of dozens, if not hundreds of traits that exist subconsciously in Tom's mind."

"I see," the defence barrister said as his eyes panned across the jury, "and where did Tom come by the will and methodology to kill two people and to attempt to kill a third, not to mention the ability to speak fluent Polish? Where did such an abomination come from?"

The translator had been told to prepare for such questions and responses and had been given instruction to not translate these to Tomasz.

"Tom Draven has been a police officer for many years. In discussion with *him,* we've been able to identify personality traits, characteristics and mannerisms for Tomasz to have – in the large part attributed to persons he has come into contact with over the course of his many investigations." The professor paused. "Tom, in fact, told me about a list he had made detailing previous investigations and commonalities, a list that has been seized into evidence by the prosecution."

"Ah yes," the barrister exclaimed, "the list my learned and esteemed colleague referred to as a *hit list.*"

"Yes, quite. In conversation with Tom we have been able to determine the origin of a number of the traits displayed," the professor explained.

"So why is Tomasz a killer then, Professor?"

"Tomasz is essentially dispensing justice," the professor paused to clear his throat. "Tomasz is *essentially* Tom, and Tom is a police officer, it's just that Tomasz exists and operates without the constraints that Tom is bound by. Tomasz is a compromise between Tom's law-abiding nature and the pure malevolence of those he has come into contact with through the course of his career."

"Have you any explanation why Tomasz chose the victims he did?"

"Well, they were all subject to various police investigations at one stage or another. I conclude that this information was openly available to Tom for whatever reason, and that the recall was made when Tomasz was the dominant persona at that given time."

"Professor, you refer to a *dominant persona,* are you able to elaborate on that for the benefit of the court, please?"

"Of course, both personas share a single mind, but only one can be dominant at any one time and therefore be in control of the host body. The dominant persona, or *Realm Primus* as it can also be known, may not be one hundred percent in control of the body, and traits of both personalities may be apparent, however both cannot be shown in the same aspect. For instance, we've proved that Tom is left-handed, yet Tomasz is right-handed; both cannot exist concurrently, it is either one of the other although switching between them can happen at any time without notice."

"So, the victims were chosen because they were under police investigation which Tom may have inadvertently researched, yet because they weren't charged or convicted Tomasz felt compelled to demand a confession before exacting justice as he saw fit?"

"Exactly, to some extent each appeared to be aware of what the other was enacting. I believe that this was how, and why, the clues that led Tom to believe he was being set up were deliberately left by him *for* he himself to find. The key ring on the shelf and the button on the ground, they appear to have been intentionally left there in such a way as to only attract Tom's attention, knowing he could be called upon to review the evidence and see the connection."

"Do you think that Tom was aware that the crimes were taking place?" the barrister asked.

"Having spoken to Tom he states he experienced the crimes being acted out in what he describes as a dream-like state."

"Thank you, Professor, I have no more questions for you at this time."

oOo

After the break for lunch, it was the prosecution's turn to cross-examine Professor White.

The prosecution gave their best attempts to dispute and disprove the Realm Primus theory and aim to convince the jury that Tom and Tomasz were one and the same.

The day and the first week of the trial ended on a disappointing note for the Crown.

DAY 133

On the first day of the second week of the trial, Tom was summoned to the stand.

He answered the questions as he was asked by both the defence and then the prosecution.

The defence's strategy was to build upon the groundwork laid by the psychological expert the previous week.

He remained oblivious in the main to what was being asked of him and responded with negative responses that outwardly began to infuriate the prosecution.

But Tom couldn't answer the questions as asked or elaborate on the accounts as he was asked to because he just didn't know.

There was no reality to Tom's responses. He made mention of fragments of an account. But it was generally spoken in the third person, as if he himself was there witnessing the events unfold as opposed to being involved with them or having any influence over them.

The result of being sat in the witness box being accused of such heinous acts regardless of motive and having absolutely no first-hand knowledge of perpetrating such crimes was taking its toll on Tom, and the emotion did start to show in his face.

Eventually, the judge stepped in and concluded the prosecution's cross-examination as they appeared to be repeatedly asking the same questions over and over expecting to either catch Tom out or to simply wear him down.

Monday ended with Tom being dismissed as a witness.

oOo

The following day, the court was adjourned because they were hopeful that it would be Tomasz sat beside his barrister, but again Tom was there, still understandably unnerved by the barrage of questions and accusations that he had been subjected to the previous day.

Tom's appearance for a second day running hadn't been unheard of, but the court was hoping to have Tomasz testify.

DAY 135

The court didn't have to wait long, as when the judge entered the courtroom the next day he saw the welcome sight of a third man sat between the defence barrister and the defendant.

After being sworn in by the by the clerk of the court, and using the translator as an intermediary, the defence began their questioning of Tomasz.

"Would you please state your name and date of birth for the record," the barrister asked.

After every question asked the translator would then address Tomasz in Polish, await his response and then convey to the court what was said.

"Tomasz Dravidas, June 20 1937," came the translated reply.

A stunned hush fell across the courtroom.

The defence was however prepared for this and continued to question Tomasz without faltering.

"How old does that make you Tomasz?"

Again, the reply came from the translator, "Thirty-six years old."

"Do you know what year this is, Tomasz?"

"Nineteen seventy-four," came the translated reply.

This was exactly what the defence was expecting Tomasz to say. They had been prepared to elaborate on this point for the benefit of the court.

The defence barrister then addressed the court. "In 1974, in the Polish city of Gdańsk, there was a case of a police officer turned vigilante. He went after those who had been acquitted, or those he believed were guilty but couldn't be proven. In total he killed six people." He paused long enough to ensure the jury had kept up. "He was never caught, instead he handed himself in and made a full confession. He has since died in prison. The defendant, Tom Draven, has studied this case, and that is perhaps where the characterisation has come from which has manifested itself in the man sitting before you today."

He could see the jury focus their attention on the man sat perfectly straight, almost to attention, in the witness box.

The defence then confirmed that Tomasz did in fact believe he was a police officer, but he admitted to knowing he was in England.

"Do you know you're on trial for the murders of Ronald Campbell and Pauline Barnes and the attempted murder of Leanne Young?"

"Yes," came the eventual reply from the translator.

"Did you commit these crimes?"

The translator was preparing to offer a translation in Polish, but what happened next stunned him as well as the rest of the courtroom.

"I – did," Tomasz replied having understood the question put to him in Polish and making his own reply in English.

The judge looked down at Tomasz, sat below him in dismay.

This response even shocked the defence who was expecting the response to come via the translator.

"Did you kill Ronald Campbell *and* Pauline Barnes *and* try to kill Leanne Young?" the defence felt he needed to repeat the question to clarify understanding.

"Yes, I did," came the reply more fluently than before.

"Why did you commit these crimes?"

"They are *not* crimes, they are punishments. They committed the crimes, I merely punished the guilty," came Tomasz' heavily accented reply.

"Why did these people need to be punished?"

"Hah! You feel that question needs to be asked?" Tomasz replied, "I ask you in what world should a paedophile, someone who kills the vulnerable for financial gain and someone who sets out to spread disease, *not* be punished? I did what you could not do. The police knew about these people and yet they did nothing. I took action and stopped the suffering, yet it is I who now stands trial."

With the confession given as expected the defence ended their questioning of Tomasz.

The prosecutor stood to take his turn before the witness. He was dumbfounded by what he had just witnessed, as a result his planned cross-examination was now completely redundant. He had but one question for the defendant. "Why did you not plead guilty at the start of this trial?"

There was a pause, the translator began to speak feeling that his services were again required.

Then Tomasz himself replied, "Because – I – was – not – asked," he said emphasising each word more than the last.

Court was adjourned for the day.

DAY 136

With a confession heard the jury would not be required to deliberate a verdict, and the prosecution and the defence would not be required to summarise the trial for their benefit by means of closing statements. All that would be required now was sentencing.

The possibility of a confession and the lines of defence were entered into discussion with the court from day one of the trial. As a result, the eventuality they found themselves facing was neither unexpected, nor unplanned for.

When court was brought into session and the judge entered the courtroom, he was hoping to have the defendant as seen the previous day stood before him.

There were no tell-tale clues as he entered, seeing only two men, the defendant and his barrister, standing at the bench.

It was only when he directly asked did he get an answer, but not the one he was hoping for.

"Sir, to who am I addressing today?" the judge asked.

"Tom Draven, My Lord," came the reply.

The judge was hoping to pass sentence on the guilty party. Knowing he was not in a position to delay sentence for an eventuality that may never come, he continued.

The court sat, and the judge reviewed aloud the relevant points of the trial.

"This has been a trial depicting some truly heinous crimes, and of a man taking it upon himself to seek out those he believed to be guilty of crimes and imposing the ultimate penalty upon them. In a civilised society, it is not down to one person to decide who is guilty and who should be punished. Whether the victims of *this* trial are innocent or guilty in their own right is not for the defendant to decide. Should the process of law find a person guilty of an offence, then under the statute of that law should they be suitably punished. As stated by one of our expert witnesses last week the specifics of this trial are rare, but not unique. I believe it has been proven that the man who stands before you today did *not* commit the crimes for which he is on trial," he paused. "The realisation is, however, that it was those hands that *did* commit these crimes, and we now know this by means of forensic evidence, but more importantly by means of a confession."

The judge then focused his gaze on the defendant, and the look of shock and horror on his face. Although Tom would have been prepared for this day, and the likely outcome, the revelation of hearing this in the judge's words still hit him hard.

"The guilty must be punished, and society needs to be spared," the judge continued.

"Please stand, sir," the judge asked, and with Tom and his barrister on their feet he continued. "Sir, it is with great regret that it is you who I am addressing today. God willing, I was hopeful that it would not be you that would be standing before me."

There was a pause and look of compassionate understanding was exchanged between the defendant and the judge.

"Do you have anything you wish to say before I pass sentence?"

"Yes, My Lord," Tom replied.

"Then, sir, please continue."

"My Lord, I still don't know how this has all has come to be. I have come to understand and accept that as a result of my actions people have died. I still don't fully understand how. It's been explained that my body committed these crimes, but not *this* mind," he said pointing to his right temple, "this mind, did not. I, Tom Draven did not kill anyone. Without the confession, I'm sure this jury would have convicted me nonetheless." He gave the jury a sideways glance. "I can only ask for the court's help, as I don't want its pity or mercy."

The judge nodded his approval of what he had just heard.

"Sir, having confessed to the crimes for which you are charged, it is the order of this court that you be sentenced to an unlimited hospital order at a facility deemed suitable for your needs, and that you remain there where you can do no more harm until such time as, upon assessment, you have been deemed safe to re-enter society."

The gavel came down.

"All rise," cried the clerk of the court.

DAY 142

"So how come I've started understanding Polish, and the other guy has started speaking English then?"

"I'm not sure yet, but there is a documented process where the once defined and segregated personas can merge, and traits become ever more apparent in the other personality, but at this point that is pure supposition," replied Tom's psychiatrist.

The sentence of an unlimited hospital order meant that the defendant would be incarcerated in a secure mental health facility until such time that the aspect of his psyche which was deemed dangerous could either be eradicated or at the very least controlled. As a result, he had been taken to an appropriate facility designed to address his specific needs. In this case he was taken to the Yew Tree Hospital, which was just outside Lincoln in the renovated buildings and grounds of a former stately home which had been sold by the owner, and then a trust, before falling into the hands of a private company.

It was Tom who had been brought here directly from court, but it was Tomasz who had actually arrived.

The staff had been told to prepare for Tom's arrival as it was he who had left the court, and as it was only a two hour transfer they expected it to still be him who arrived. But at some point during the journey, Tom had taken a nap and it was Tomasz who had awakened for the arrival.

As the final week of the trial had illustrated, there was no exact science or way to predict any eventuality when it came to who would be the dominant persona on any given occasion.

In the days since his arrival at the hospital, he had remained as Tomasz, and today was the first day of Tom's re-emergence. Therefore, today also marked the first consultation with Tom, as Tomasz had already been introduced to the staff. As it turned out there was no further need for a translator.

This apparent mergence caused his psychiatrist concern.

"The language ability may be the only trait currently visible, but we should be prepared for other traits to soon become apparent."

"Such as?" Tom queried.

"Personality and behaviour," came the reply, "tolerance or intolerance, and aggression."

Tom didn't like the idea of this, he was already uneasy with the idea that his dreams had already manifest themselves in another's reality, and vice versa.

"And you need to be prepared in that these traits may well be extenuated by the treatment, at least initially."

"What do you mean?" Tom replied with concern.

"We propose to address the transference between the personas by focusing on how the switch between them takes place. The door we've identified at present opens during your sleep, so that's where we'll focus our efforts. Initially, we will medicate you to prevent you from having dreams."

"And if that doesn't work?" Tom asked looking concerned.

"Then maybe we can try hypnosis and should that be unsuccessful, then we can always consider sleep deprivation," came the reply.

oOo

Following the consultation, Tom was given an official tour of the hospital and its facilities. His tour guide was a large man, much taller than Tom, who failed to introduce himself, but that Tom could see by his name badge to be Malcolm.

Yew Tree Hospital was a privately funded trust facility which meant it was outside of the remit of the already overstretched National Health Service or Her Majesty's Prison Service.

Someone had evidently seen there was a profit to be made in privately funded mental health care and was speculating to accumulate.

The hospital complex consisted of a number of buildings, some of which residents had access to, and others which of were solely administration. The site itself had been greatly expanded in the time since it ceased being a stately home. The original home itself was now the entrance and reception, as well as the main administration block. However, there were a number of residents housed within this building which also contained the treatment rooms.

This was a state-of-the-art facility. Long gone were the days of a jangling bunch of keys hanging from a staff member's belt loop. Here it was much more sophisticated; a proximity card allowed the doors to open without any contact between a card and a sensor. This was similar to the keyless entry and ignition of many prestige cars, where the doors unlocked just by approaching the vehicle.

As Tom was escorted around he was impressed how some doors opened and others didn't. He enquired how this was differentiated. This was explained to him as being due to the fact that there was a proximity sensor on both sides of the door frame and the pass card needed to be equally situated between both sensors for the door to react. This was translated to mean should a pass card be simply passing a doorway on one side or the other then the sensors would differentiate this from someone approaching the door and pausing in front of it, "Of course, like any system, it's not perfect," the explanation concluded. But in principle it worked. Malcolm also explained that his card would have access to certain areas as he did not have the necessary clearance.

To further illustrate his explanation, Malcolm showed Tom his card. The proximity card itself was worn inside the staff member's uniform thus preventing it from being snatched by a resident to facilitate an escape.

In addition to the original building being renovated and extended, the extensive grounds that came with the house had been modified and secured. The perimeter wall had been upgraded to prevent people from getting out, in addition to just stopping those from getting in. Also, an inner boundary was created, and it was within this boundary that the residents had freedom to roam. The grounds between the two barriers was a no man's land. After all, this was a facility to house criminals, so it was essentially run as a prison, although those detained were commonly referred to as residents, and the guards were more sympathetically referred to as staff members, or *staff* when it came to the residents addressing them.

The differences between a standard prison and this facility were numerous and obvious. There were still walls and locked doors, but the feel was entirely different to that Tom had experienced prior to the trial.

During the tour, Tom was given information about the facility and the requirements of the residents. Even with restrictions, he was still allowed greater freedom than had been afforded him previously.

It was explained that he could have free rein of the grounds during designated times should he so desire. The hospital did have a limited gym facility, as well as a staffed physiotherapy department.

Malcolm also explained how the hospital got its name, after the many yew trees that were evident along the approach road. Originally, part of the home's grounds consisted of a small cemetery of the ancestral family which had since been exhumed.

The yew tree is the symbol of the immortality of the soul, this comes from pre-Christian beliefs and customs of the Celt druids. Yews were planted around Pagan temples much before the Christian times, being later adopted by the Church as a holy symbol. Still today, yews are planted in British graveyards.

It became apparent to Tom as the tour continued around the grounds, that at no point could outside civilisation be seen or even heard. The only indicator that humanity existed beyond the walls and gates was the occasional passenger jet flying overhead. For all intents and purposes, this could quite easily have been the last bastion of life on the planet.

Tom didn't even know whereabouts in England this facility was. He had not been aware of the journey and certainly hadn't seen any landmarks to pinpoint his location roughly on a map.

"That's the way we like it," replied Malcolm when asked, "so much so that all visitors enter into a confidentiality agreement prior to this location being disclosed and any visitation granted."

This puzzled Tom, to him this was just another prison, albeit one with better facilities and nicer grounds, but still a prison.

Throughout the tour when another resident was seen they were introduced by first name only. It was almost as if they didn't want the residents to know too much about one another. This suited Tom just fine as he'd gone to great lengths to protect his unique status in prison.

"How many do you have here at any one time?"

"Max number is fifty, only got about half that at the mo," Malcolm replied.

"Is this a single-sex facility?" Tom then asked.

"Nope," Malcolm replied, "we do have ladies here too, but they're in another wing, and their grounds are segregated. You won't see any, so you can get the idea of any funny business out of your head. There are some rather fine ladies on staff to keep your heart racing though, but it's strictly look and don't touch, and that goes for us too."

Tom was starting to feel that this was all very *One Flew Over The Cuckoo's Nest*, and so far, all he'd need to see would be Nurse Ratched. He asked his questions partly out of idle curiosity but mainly to keep the conversation going and breaking up the monotony of the tour. He didn't have any interest whatsoever in any interaction with fellow residents or staff, not in the way Malcolm was suggesting anyway.

Tom was hoping that contact had been made with Jess and that her vetting was being processed, and that she would be arranging a visit.

As if psychic, Malcolm said, "Visits can be any day up until eight p.m., at the director's discretion, of course. Any breaches of the rules or disciplinary issues can result in visits being cancelled, okay? You follow the rules and treat us as you want us to treat you then we'll all get along just fine." He paused. "But you fuck with us and you may not even be here long enough to regret it."

Tom slowed his pace to allow what had just been said to sink in. He didn't feel the need to be threatened in such a way. The fact that he had infuriated him. His escort noticed that Tom had fallen behind him.

"You got a problem with that?"

Tom just shook his head and quickened his pace to catch up. If all the staff were the same as this one, it would certainly make for an interesting indefinite term here he thought.

After the tour of the grounds, they went back inside where the tour concluded in the familiar surroundings of what Tom had already seen of the dining area and communal leisure rooms.

"A couple of last things." Malcolm paused long enough to ensure he had Tom's attention. "No personal items outside, okay, anything we issue you is fine, but nothing else. Do you smoke?"

Tom reluctantly nodded. "Well you're gonna have to have one of these then."

Malcolm took a lighter from his pocket, flipped open the top and activated it. A small arc of electricity illuminated between the terminals. To Tom, it looked like a miniaturised TASER.

"This is what you've gotta have, no flames. They've got a supply of them, so your one can be swapped out." Malcolm paused. "Tell you what, here, you have this one, I'll get myself a replacement, save you the hassle."

He handed the lighter to Tom who gratefully received it.

"That's us done, the rest you'll pick up in time," Malcolm said, "but anything else you wanna know, just ask, okay?"

That parting gesture and remark were a million miles away from the intimidating comment he had made earlier about not *fucking with us*.

Good Cop, Bad Cop all rolled into one, Tom thought momentarily before dismissing it from his mind. He was grateful about the lighter, that was one less thing he needed to concern himself about.

What with the consultation and the tour it had been a long and exhausting day for Tom. So, although he had freedom to go about the communal areas of the hospital as he so desired, all he desired right now was to go back to his room and lie down.

DAY 154

"So how are they treating you in here then, is it any better than that shit hole they kept you in before the trial?"

"Oh, it's way better, it's like a fucking holiday camp here," Tom replied.

Tom sat with his long-time friend and colleague Carl in the visitor's wing of the hospital. It was a spacious and airy room with bi-folding doors that led out onto a paved courtyard, giving the party a choice in fine weather to stay indoors or sit outside. It didn't have the oppressive feel to it that the prison visitor's suite had. Gone were the bolted-down tables and chairs and guards on every exit. It did have staff members on hand but until needed they kept themselves occupied and the party didn't feel in any way oppressed.

Because the vetting procedure was much more stringent, and visitors were subjected to greater scrutiny upon entering the facility they were rewarded with greater freedom once inside.

"I'm sorry I haven't been able to see you before now; did Jess tell you why? That we all were given a blanket ban on seeing you?" said Carl.

"Well, she did mention something about it when she visited me in prison," Tom replied. "So, it's all true then, *you* actually didn't do it?" Carl asked.

"Yes and no, to be quite honest I don't fucking understand it, even when I've got some poxy so-called expert telling me how it is, I don't wanna believe it. How can I accept that I've got a killer lurking inside me, how can I?" He paused. "Would you?"

"How did this even happen?" Carl asked.

"The fucking hypnosis I had to quit smoking triggered an accumulation of suppressed character traits which supposedly came together to form a personality. I mean for fuck's sake I'm supposed to be a killer cop from the 1970s just because I wrote a fucking thesis on the guy back in uni."

"Can they help you?" Carl asked.

"I'm on mood suppressants at the mo, but if that doesn't work they're considering a deeper hypnosis to go back and supposedly close what they're calling a doorway between the personalities. They've also mentioned sleep deprivation." There was another pause. "Essentially they haven't got the first fucking clue what to do."

"Sleep deprivation? How will that help?"

"Apparently, I switch personalities when I'm asleep, should I dream about one then I wake up as them. I've had to complete a questionnaire every morning since the beginning of the trial asking me about my dreams. At first there were two copies, one in English, the other in Polish, now I just get an English copy. The meds are meant to stop me from dreaming. I've supposedly been *me* for a few days now, and the *other guy* hasn't made an appearance since I've arrived here, even though it wasn't me who arrived here." Tom chuckled at having confused both Carl and himself.

"Well if all this works you can get out of here then, is that right?"

"Pretty much," replied Tom with a look of hope on his face. "Y'know I haven't seen Jess since before the trial, how is she?"

"As far as I know she's doing fine, she's planning to come up here when she's been cleared. I got done sooner as I needed less vetting. She'll be here as soon as she can."

"Y'know, I don't even know where fucking *here* is?" Tom explained, "I dunno why this place needs to be such a big fucking secret?"

"Well, all I can tell you is it's near Lincoln, but that's it, I'm not telling you any more, so don't ask," Carl replied, "if you knew who this place has housed over the years you'd want this place to be a big secret too."

Carl gave Tom a look to over-emphasise exactly what he was talking about, and Tom mirrored the look and nodded upon realising what Carl was getting at.

This facility would have undoubtedly housed and treated the very worst of the criminally insane that the country had to offer. Not all at once, and probably none right now, but this was meant to treat the untreatable, and should they remain untreatable to at least keep them hidden away and keep society safe. From the inside, it appeared to be fairly lenient on security, but Tom felt that beyond the immediate vicinity of the building was where the real security lay.

"Do you wanna go outside?" Tom asked. It was a lovely sunny day, and as they had the freedom and choice whether or not to stay inside Tom felt the desire to be outside. He collected up a notebook and pen that he had placed in front of him on the table.

"What's with the pad and pen?" Carl enquired.

"Oh," Tom began, not quite knowing how best to explain this to Carl, "it's for free writing, I'm supposed to have this with me all day, every day, and should the need occur to me to write something then I'm meant to open my mind and let it flow onto paper, or something like that."

Free writing is a prewriting technique in which the subject writes continuously for a set period of time, or in Tom's case whenever the urge took him, with regard to spelling, grammar or topic. It is designed to produce raw, often unusable material, but again in Tom's case it was designed to act as an insight into his subconscious, define which personality was dominant at any given time. He was required to submit the pad to his psychiatrist after any and all periods of writing.

The doors from the visitor's wing were open and led to the enclosed courtyard to allow the residents and their visitors to smoke as well as enjoy fresh air.

Once outside, Tom tucked his pad under his arm and took a pouch of tobacco from his pocket, he took out a single paper from a packet and held it between his lips as he replaced the papers. He then took a pinch of tobacco from the pouch and began moulding it along the paper. He looked up to see a disapproving look from Carl.

The look was hardly unexpected. Following all the determination and previous attempts to quit smoking, not to mention that the most recent attempt and its methods had apparently resulted in this conversation taking place in this facility hidden somewhere in the British Isles. His friend and colleague had started smoking *again.*

Tom gave an unashamed and defiant look in return. "What do you expect?" he said.

Carl didn't have an answer and just shrugged his shoulders. He could see the point Tom had made.

Tom fashioned a now expertly rolled cigarette, and not something that resembled a Nik-Nak crisp as his earlier efforts had.

Tom turned to put his back to the breeze that he could feel so he could light the cigarette.

He took a long slow satisfying drag. He knew what Carl's look was based on, he looked at the cigarette smouldering in his fingers and realised the trouble it had caused.

Quitting is just as dangerous as smoking, he thought.

The courtyard was a sizeable area. There were other residents there with their visitors, but they all gave each other enough space to not be privy to any other conversations beyond their own.

"It's fucking bizarre here," Tom began, "no one talks to anyone, I've been here a couple of weeks now and I've hardly said two words to anyone. In prison, all you had was conversation but here it's practically non-existent. No one knows anyone either, all anyone is referred to is by their first name, even the staff. Never known anything like it."

"How're you feeling in yourself?" Carl asked.

"Dunno, I've been told I've done all this stuff, but I still can't bring myself to truly believe any of it. The fucking trial was the worst of it though, standing there being sentenced, being told I'd made a confession which I had no recollection of, I was screaming inside with no one to hear me."

"Well, if you need anything from me you know where to find me, okay, I'll be back up when I can. Just play along with everything and get yourself out of here, that's all you *can* do."

They both spent the remainder of the visit in the courtyard. When time was called they shook hands before Carl pulled his friend in for a hug which ended with him pulling away and turning immediately so that Tom never got to see his face before he walked off back inside before heading towards the exit.

Tom remained outside in the courtyard. He rolled himself another cigarette. He held the finished item in his hand and stared at it for several moments before throwing it to the ground in disgust and dragging his foot across it. A look of anger came over his face, a now all too familiar sight.

DAY 159

Tom awoke to find his room stripped of all personal items. He hadn't accumulated all that much in the few weeks he had been at Yew Trees but what he had was now gone. For him, personal possessions consisted of his tobacco pouch, lighter and his writing pad. But regardless everything was gone.

Also, he ached all over. He felt like he had overdone it at the gym and not stretched afterwards. Standing up was going to hurt.

He got up and went over to the door. He was right, getting up did hurt, gone was the fluid movement, everything was slow and clunky and came with a sound effect. Once upright he slowly and cautiously shuffled over to the door. He felt at any time his body would fail him as it hurt so much. He turned the doorknob and pulled. Nothing happened, he pushed, still nothing.

This door was normally locked overnight with an electromagnet, but during the day it should be unlocked. This lock allowed for rooms to be entered at any time, but only during unrestricted times can residents exit their rooms.

Tom was not sure what the time was because even the travel style alarm clock had been taken from beside his bed. But it was daylight, and bright enough to suggest that the sun was up. Tom couldn't tell for sure as the window was frosted much like a bathroom window.

Beside the door was an intercom panel. He pressed the *call* button. After a few seconds, a voice crackled on the speaker.

"Yes," came the reply.

"What's going on?" Tom enquired, "where's all my stuff gone?"

"Wait there, we'll have someone come down to speak to you."

"Wait right here, where the fuck do you expect me to go?"

Tom wasn't able to determine just how long he had to wait, but it felt like an age.

He could hear activity on the other side of the door. Then a voice could be heard addressing him through it.

"Tom, please can you sit on the bed where we can see you?"

He had never been asked to do this before someone entered his room, but nothing about today was familiar. In order to get to the bottom of what was going on, he felt he needed to comply. For a moment Malcolm's warning echoed in his mind, *you fuck with us and you may be here long enough to regret it, you get me?*

Tom sat as requested. He felt as if every move he made was now being observed through the spyhole in the door. The door then opened.

In stepped two members of staff and his psychiatrist. One of the staff members was carrying what looked to Tom like a set of restraints. From Tom's time in the police, he had seen numerous restraints used in custody for those determined to self-harm or lash out at officers. He was no expert on the subject, but they did look familiar.

"Tom, do we need to restrain you?" his psychiatrist asked. Simultaneously the staff member held up the restraints as if his mere holding them to his side in plain view wasn't sufficient.

"Umm, no!" Tom exclaimed unable to comprehend what was happening.

"I'm glad to hear that, Tom, will you come with us please?"

Tom cautiously rose to his feet again. He hurt less than before, although it did still come with a sound effect.

Once again, he was familiar with this scenario, he knew any sudden movements could be considered as an act of aggression, and the staff members would most likely jump on him, wrestle him to the floor before strapping him into the restraints.

Tom wanted answers, and the way to achieve that in the quickest possible way would be to be passive and compliant.

Once outside of his room Tom saw yet another two staff members waiting in the corridor, one of them was Malcolm. Tom was dwarfed in between them all as they escorted him down the corridor.

Dead man walking, Tom thought, remembering back to too many crime and punishment films he'd watched with the condemned man surrounded by guards on his final walk.

They passed through several secure doors before turning into a wing that Tom had never entered before. He became increasingly unsettled.

Eventually, they turned into a room. Luckily, the room was large enough for them all to enter with space to spare. Malcolm and one other then stepped outside so all that remained were the two staff members who had originally entered Tom's room.

Tom was sat on a chair in front of a desk, his psychiatrist had circled the desk to stand opposite him, he stood next to a seated man who remained silent. The two staff members stood back from Tom's chair on either side. Tom could no longer see them, but he knew they were still there.

Tom still didn't know what the time was. He felt it must've been late morning as the sun was still low in the sky, its rays cutting a beam directly through the window into Tom's face. The psychiatrist could see Tom squinting and acted sympathetically by closing one curtain to shield Tom whilst still allowing enough sun in to light the room.

"What brings us here today, Tom?" his psychiatrist asked.

The question was vague, and Tom found it impossible to answer, the only response that occurred to him was one of sarcasm, but he felt that wasn't wholly appropriate.

"I was hoping you could shed some light for us," his psychiatrist continued.

Again, given his previous sympathetic actions, only sarcasm and a witticism occurred to Tom. As a result, he sat there silent.

His eyes, having now adjusted to the room, allowed for greater clarity of those across from him. He recognised his psychiatrist, but the man sat next to him, dressed in a suit, elbows on the desk, hands clasped covering the lower part of his face, he had never seen before.

Thinking of his potential responses caused a smile to fall across Tom's face.

His psychiatrist saw his reaction. "This isn't a laughing matter, Tom."

With that, he picked up what resembled a TV remote control from the desk and pressed a button which caused a bright light to illuminate from Tom's right. He turned to face it. It was a TV hidden in the darkness outside of the sun's rays.

When the image became clear Tom could see that it was CCTV footage. The date/time stamp showed that it was from just before ten p.m., presumably the previous evening, but Tom couldn't be sure.

Ten p.m. is when the electromagnetic locks are activated keeping the residents in their rooms overnight.

The footage was of good quality and showed a full colour image. It showed a hospital corridor, one of the residential wings. After running on what appeared to be a still image, things started to happen. It wasn't a still image though, as the clock in the corner kept counting.

At 21:55:14 hrs a figure was seen to enter the frame from the right-hand side. Tom's psychiatrist paused the footage at this point. The figure appeared to be a male, he was dressed in dark coloured jogging trousers and a grey polo style shirt and had a tattoo or bruising extending below the left sleeve of his shirt.

The psychiatrist looked at Tom to see his reaction, when none came he pressed play again.

The footage went on to show the male approach the middle of three doors exiting off the side of the corridor. As he took hold of the handle he looked back in the direction he had come.

Again, the footage is paused and the figure in the image could clearly be seen to be that of Tom.

Tom sat forward in his chair. The footage showed him, but he had no idea of where exactly it was, why he was there or what was coming next, although all of it presumably happened late last night.

The footage was started again. At 21:55:22 hrs a figure was then seen to enter the room beyond the middle door, and the door was allowed to close.

The footage continued, the clock counting on, but time stood still for Tom, sitting in the office in the here and now.

At 21:59:07 hrs the door opened, and the same figure stepped out into the corridor again, allowing the door to close by itself. The figure then exited the frame to the right in the direction he had come from at 21:59:12 hrs.

The psychiatrist then turned the TV off and set the remote control back on the desk.

"What can you tell me about what you've just seen then, Tom?" he asked.

Tom was bewildered, he had absolutely no recollection of what he had just witnessed.

"Whose room was that?" Tom asked.

"That," — the psychiatrist paused — "is another matter we need to discuss. But first things first."

"Show me your hands would you please, Tom?"

Tom looked at the palms of his hands, they were trembling but there was nothing there to suggest anything untoward.

He then slowly and cautiously turned them over. They were bruised and swollen with fresh abrasions and laceration injuries.

"What the fuck?" Tom muttered to himself.

"Let me see," came the request from behind the desk.

Tom held his hands up, backs towards the window, the sunlight showing off his injuries.

"And just how did that happen, Tom?"

Tom shook his head. "I don't know," he replied.

"From all accounts, Tom, you were *you* yesterday, no accent, perfect English, the free writing you submitted throughout the day indicated you were *you*, Tom Draven, and then this, and you say you have no recollection?"

Tom turned to look at the backs of his hands in disbelief and shook his head.

"I really don't know, I don't know about any of this. I don't know whose room that is, I don't know where that room is, I don't know how I got these injuries, and I sure as hell don't know what went on behind that fucking door."

"Okay, Tom, just settle down," the psychiatrist replied, "I'll tell you exactly what happened behind that door."

He paused and opened a cardboard wallet on the desk. From it he took out some photographic images.

"This is what *you* did behind that door," he said as he laid the images across the front of the desk so that Tom could see them.

Tom went to stand up, so he could move closer to the desk, but in an instant, he felt a hand on his shoulder pushing him down, back down into his chair. The pressure of the hand caused him pain, so he complied. Having recomposed himself, he sat tall in his chair, so he could lean forward as close to the desk as he could to make sense of what he was being shown.

The images were intended to be viewed from left to right and showed a room in disarray, then a close-up of a bed with bloodied sheets and a pillow. The remaining images showed a beaten, bloodied and bandaged man lying in a different bed, a clean bed, Tom presumed an infirmary or medical hospital bed.

He didn't recognise the man, he may have done previously, but his injuries prevented any immediate recognition.

Tom sat silent. The man sitting across from him remained silent, he had now leant back in his chair, his face now completely hidden, silhouetted by the rays of sunshine entering the room directly behind him. His inactivity was unsettling for Tom.

"He's lucky to be alive," the seated man began. "Extensive injuries to the head and neck. He was so badly injured that he had an air ambulance fly him to the nearest hospital with an emergency department. The full extent of his injuries is not yet known. To be honest they don't know how he made it through the night."

Tom looked dumbfounded. He was having a horrible feeling of déjà vu all over again.

The seated man again leant forward and put his forearms on the desk.

Seeing that Tom was appearing to be more perplexed by who he was, as opposed to what he had just said, he felt an introduction was in order.

"Tom, I am Alexander Waldwin, I am the director of this facility. You may be wondering why you are still here. This matter has not been reported to the police. As you are no doubt aware, children under the age of ten years of age are deemed to not be criminally responsible for their actions. Well, those here are no longer deemed responsible for their actions. They have been deemed by the state to be beyond any social responsibility. Hence calling the police would be futile and a waste of everyone's time. This will be dealt with internally, and I want you to assure me of your complete cooperation with your treatment or things can quite easily change here for you. Do you understand me?"

Tom had lost all sense of the words that the director was now saying to him. For now, he was lost in his own world. Was this the realisation that the treatment they had initially pinned their hopes to, the treatment that was his best hope for leaving this place and returning to something of a normal life was failing, that he was still experiencing his duality and that people were still at risk?

"Tom... TOM," his psychiatrist called.

Suddenly Tom was back in the moment.

"I have something else I want you to see, Tom."

Once again, his psychiatrist had picked up the remote control from the desk and again turned on the TV. This time the image was of another corridor and doorway. Above the doorway was a sign that read NO UNAUTHORISED PERSONS ALLOWED. The date/time stamp was two days prior to the previous footage, so Tom was presuming this footage was three days old.

The time stamp showed 19:42:11 hrs. As the footage played, the door below the sign was seen to open inwards. Then out from behind the door, and out into the corridor stepped a figure. As the figure cleared the doorway, and the door closed behind him the footage was paused. This was the clearest frame to show the figure to the camera.

The figure again looked identical to Tom.

Again, Tom professed his innocence. He stated he did not know where this door was or what was beyond it.

"I'll tell you what's beyond it," the psychiatrist said, "beyond that door is our records wing. Beyond that door are all of our patient records. How did you know that, and how did you get in there?"

Tom sat there silent, unable to verbalise a response.

"We don't know either," the director added, "you're not shown entering that wing, there's no audited access using any key cards, how did you do it?"

Tom just shrugged his shoulders and raised his hands in dismay.

The director then went back into the same cardboard wallet that had contained the photographs and took out a sheet of printed paper.

"I have here an audit log of all the patient records accessed in the time immediately prior to *you* exiting the records room. You knew exactly what you were looking for, you were looking for the true identities of the those here, and why they are here, weren't you? The only thing we can't figure out is how?"

Tom felt all the eyes in the room burning him from all angles.

"And then you went to carry on the work which you had started on the outside, didn't you?" his psychiatrist added.

Tom felt the question was rhetorical so didn't offer any reply.

"And you chose the one patient who was stated to have no means of cure or treatment, a terminally insane case. And you punished him, didn't you? How many more, Tom, how many more? You can't kill them all!"

There was a silence, Tom felt this was his opportunity to say something.

"I did…" he began.

"Didn't do it, of course you didn't, you didn't do any of it, did you, Tom, anything wrong happens and it's always going to be the other guy, isn't it Tom, when are you going to take some responsibility f —?"

The director felt as if the psychiatrist was on the verge of saying too much and stopped him mid-sentence.

"We're done here, take him back to his room," the director said.

oOo

After being taken back to his room Tom decided he need some fresh air, he needed space as for the first time was feeling claustrophobic in his room despite having more room there than ever before having had all his possessions removed.

The sun was now high in the sky when he stepped outside. He felt its warmth on his face and felt peace within him. For a moment, it was like nothing mattered. But that was not the case.

Tom had faced the reality that once again his hands had come close to taking yet another life, and yet again he knew nothing of it and had absolutely no control in order to prevent it.

As he walked the grounds he pondered this dilemma. He relived the footage of him shown on CCTV and the images of the injuries he had caused. As he walked he looked down at his hands and saw the injuries that he had himself sustained.

It had been explained that his treatment was experimental, very much trial and error. Being medicated didn't appear to eliminate or suppress the rage and desire from within, what if the hypnosis would prove unsuccessful too?

Tom felt he needed to come up with a fall-back option himself. But in the confines of the hospital, his options and resources were severely limited.

oOo

Tom had been outside longer than he had expected to be. So much so that he had missed the midday meal. Then when found not to be in his room, staff were actively searching for him. As it turned out it was Malcolm who spotted Tom.

Tom was seen crouching under a tree, one of the trees by which the hospital earned its name. He appeared to be scratching around in the dirt beneath the tree, brushing twigs and leaves to one side as if searching for something in particular.

"Ah, there you are," said Malcolm, "thought we'd lost you. Are you okay?"

Still crouched Tom turned to look up at Malcolm who towered over him. He smiled and stood up and brushed his hands together causing dirt to fall from them.

"Come on, back we go," Malcolm said as he gestured back towards the buildings, "you've been out here so long you've missed lunch. Are you hungry, can sort you a sandwich if you are?"

Malcolm paused briefly to allow Tom to get a couple of steps ahead of him. Much like the detention officers in police custody, they were trained not to have a patient walk behind them as it makes them vulnerable to an attack. As Tom walked he could feel Malcolm's eyes on him, checking to see if he had secreted anything he may have found in the grounds.

Their clothes of polo shirts and joggers gave limited options when it came to hiding anything sizeable.

oOo

Having come back inside, and no longer under Malcolm's watchful eye, it was now a case of deciding what to do with what he had in fact collected.

Tom couldn't leave the items in his room as patients were subjected to regular checks, and no unsolicited articles are allowed to be kept in his room. Only his smoking materials and writing pad were allowed to be kept overnight in addition to other approved items.

Tom had a look around the communal recreation areas, looking for somewhere suitable. Then it dawned on him; the library.

The hospital library wasn't a library per se, just a couple of bookcases fixed to the wall in the communal hub. There was a TV there and a couple of sofas. This was essentially the social centre of the hospital for residents should they desire the company or entertainment. Often there were residents there at any time of the day, but conversation was minimal, if non-existent.

All of the books were paperbacks, and all of the magazines had their staples removed to prevent any self-harming or fashioning of weapons.

Tom took an interested glance along the spines of the first shelf, all looked like they had been well used. He didn't want someone to accidentally stumble across his treasure, so he was looking for a book that didn't appear to be popular.

On a lower shelf, he found what he was looking for. The spine was intact and stood out by that fact alone.

Tom took the book from the shelf. He admired the cover art, the cover showed a male figure descending some steps in hues of blue and white. He read the sub-title, this caught his interest. He turned the book over and read the synopsis on the back cover.

"Ah," he exclaimed. It was a story about a rogue cop. That would probably explain why it wasn't proving a popular read among the residents. It had probably been brought in having been read by a member of staff.

The synopsis got Tom's approval. "Looks good, might get around to reading this myself if I'm here long enough."

Tom then flicked to some middle pages and again his curiosity got the better of him. His mind wandered from the task at hand as he started to read a couple of paragraphs.

Remembering why he had picked up the book in the first place, he turned to have his back to the shelves and glanced across the room. There were some comings and goings, but no one was taking the slightest notice of him.

Tom held his place in the book with one hand whilst reaching into the pocket of his trousers with the other. He pulled out what he had collected from the grounds and placed it between the pages. He then closed the book ensuring the shape was not distorted by what it was now hiding and placed it back on the lowest shelf.

Tom then continued to peruse the higher shelves and found a well-fingered biography of a notorious criminal. He took this from the shelf to give his task a publicised purpose and retired to one of the sofas and began to read.

He spent the rest of the afternoon in the company of other patients, before having his evening meal and heading back to his room. He was hoping to find that his possessions had been returned. Alas, he was to be disappointed.

DAY 173

"I don't know just how much more of this I can handle," Tom said.

During the course of the last two weeks, two things had happened. Firstly, Jess had finally had her vetting result come back meaning she could now visit Tom, and secondly due to the revelation which resulted in a fellow patient being hospitalised it became brutally apparent that the medication that Tom had previously been administered was deemed ineffective. It had been decided to move onto a more invasive process in an attempt to deal with the issue at hand.

The more invasive process involved hypnosis. Tom had already undergone hypnosis. That had been deemed as the cause for all that had happened since.

This process, however, was designed to go deeper than anything that had taken place previously, and as a result, the intention would be to attempt to undo every bit of damage that had been done previously.

It was stated in court that the aforementioned process, a process designed to assist Tom in quitting smoking had caused a doorway in his mind to be left open. Through this doorway, dormant personality traits were allowed to emerge.

This doorway also formed a barrier between the personalities and only allowed each a glimpse of the other. However, the doorway was becoming wider and wider, allowing more of each personality to be prevalent in the other. It was also deemed a possibility that the door now ceased to close thus allowing both personalities to be apparent at any given time.

This was happening at an ever-increasing level. However, none of this was consistent. Sometimes, one would be wholly aware of what the other had done, bearing witness to it sometimes in great detail, yet on other occasions, such as Tom being made aware that his alter-ego had breached the security of the administration block and gained unauthorised access to patient records, he had absolutely no cognitive memory of it.

This lack of recollection was now starting to infuriate his psychiatrist. He was no longer willing to believe that Tom could merely be an innocent spectator. This was not the case; the situation was much more erratic and unpredictable than that. Just as no one could predict which personality was dominant when he woke, neither could they determine what level of control each could have over the other.

The treatment itself seemed to be progressing well. The daily session consisted of the hypnotherapist probing each personality regardless of who it was, asking questions about their origin, what they knew and why they were behaving as they had been.

When it came to Tom, the traits were believed and nurtured, however when it came to Tomasz, he was told his traits were decreed as false and to cease behaving in this way.

At this early stage, it was impossible to determine if there was any positive effect brought on by the treatment. But one thing was becoming evident, and that was that both personalities were becoming increasingly hostile, not only towards each other, but externally too. A number of reports had come in stating belligerent behaviour towards staff and fellow residents. Added to which, Tomasz was becoming ever more proficient at speaking English. In that respect, it was becoming increasingly difficult to tell them apart. Also, the free writing exercises were being submitted from each, now without distinction as to whether they were being exclusively written by one hand or the other.

The most recent reported incident during the previous few days where Malcolm had reported being accosted by one of them in the grounds. It only involved verbal threats, but Malcolm was unable to determine which one, Tom or Tomasz, was making the threats. There was nothing immediately evident to determine who was in control at that given moment. Also, given the fact that it was perhaps intentionally out of the coverage of any CCTV there was no opportunity to review the incident to determine any characteristics.

This matter was certainly brought to Tom's attention when it was evident that he was in control during his first therapy session following the incident. Once again, and as predicted by his psychiatrist, Tom claimed to have absolutely no knowledge of the incident.

Tom was unsure if Tomasz had been approached about the incident. He was also unsure if and when he was missing days any more. In a place with a strictly regimented schedule each day could easily merge into the next, resulting in the possibility that a day or two could be missed altogether. Maybe this was being allowed to happen, maybe the staff were intentionally not advising him of any missing days, even if they were aware themselves?

Tom decided he had to take this matter into his own hands since being made aware of the incident involving Malcolm. Tom used to sleep each night in his underwear, and possibly a polo shirt if he was chilly. However, in order to determine whether or not he was missing a day here or there, he decided to start sleeping naked. Then every morning when he would wake up he would intentionally put his underwear on inside-out. This way he would be aware that should Tomasz emerge, he would revert to habit and continue to sleep with his underpants on, and potentially with them being worn correctly. This way Tom felt he would realise any omissions upon waking as himself and finding himself wearing correctly worn underwear. This would mean that he had spent time previously as Tomasz and be prepared for any consequences.

oOo

Jess sat there aghast, she couldn't believe what she was hearing. It was a lot to take in, after all she hadn't seen Tom since before the trail which was over two months earlier, and before the psychiatric professionals gave their opinion in court during the trial.

She started to cry, Tom tried his best to console her.

"They did explain to me before any of this treatment that this might happen," Tom said.

However, they hadn't done a good job of explaining it, and he didn't believe it any more than he expected Jess to. "It's all part of the process apparently, that's why I'm here so I'm safe, and everyone's safe while this plays out."

Tom wasn't convincing and in turn neither was Jess. Sitting across from her was the man she loved, yet in him, she saw less and less of the man she fell in love with.

Tom had grown distant. He had always been analytical but had never metaphorically dissected himself before.

She was beginning to see a distinct difference in him, things she didn't recognise, things that scared her.

For the remainder of the visit they tried to distract themselves from the reality of the situation by hypothesising about life after the hospital, holidays to be had, and how things were at home.

It did little to distract them, and before Jess left they found themselves back on the original subject. Tom didn't want this, Jess didn't want this, but it was the only subject that had any meaning for either of them right now.

"We can get through this, y'know that, don't you?" she asked. Now the roles were reversed, but Jess was no more convinced than she was trying to make Tom.

"Of course, we can," he said with a reassuring look of determination.

This allowed them both to feel momentarily at ease.

At the end of the visitor's session they stood and hugged with Jess leaving a single kiss on his cheek before she turned and walked back inside the visitor's wing.

DAY 181

This morning Tom woke a little later than normal. Without his alarm clock beside the bed, he was unsure what the exact time was. He could hear activity in the corridor. An unusual amount had it been before curfew, so he deduced he had overslept. As a result, he got dressed in a hurry and left his room in order to make it down to the canteen hoping to still be in time for breakfast.

Today was the highlight of his week because today he was due his now weekly visitor. This week Carl would be taking his turn to make the journey up to see him.

Having made it in time to enjoy a hearty breakfast, he was then able to slow things down a bit. He went to the toilets and freshened up and made the best effort possible with what was available in order to prepare himself for his guest.

Tom sat in the common area of the TV lounge watching the clock. When it eventually clicked around to a few minutes to the appointed hour Tom headed down towards the courtyard to be booked in for his visit.

He liked to arrive early to get a good table and be there ready for his guest. He didn't like the idea of having to rush in the hope of getting a good spot, and he certainly didn't want his guest to arrive before him and sit there waiting, possibly worrying.

Tom approached the staff member waiting at the entrance to the courtyard. He was identical in appearance to all the other members of staff scattered around the hospital, except for the fact that he held a clipboard which had a register of the residents who had visitors each day.

Tom didn't know this staff member, so he naturally assumed that the staff member wouldn't know him either, so he introduced himself.

"Good morning. Tom Draven," he said, introducing himself to the staff member.

"Morning, Tom," the staff member said. He looked at Tom and then lowered his glance to view the list on his clipboard.

"Draven, Draven, Draven," he whispered to himself as he looked down the list of names on the clipboard.

Tom could see his glance go from top to bottom, then back to the top and down the list for a second and third time.

"I'm sorry, Tom," he said eventually admitting defeat, "I don't see your name down here for today."

Tom looked puzzled. "But I've had visits booked for every Friday since I got here."

"It's Saturday today, Tom," the staff member said matter-of-factly. He could then see a look of confusion engulf Tom's face.

The staff member then lifted the top few pages on the clipboard. He scanned the pages beneath. After a few seconds, he spoke to Tom.

"You're right, you were down for a visit *yesterday*, a Carl Wainwright signed in to see you," he said.

"And, where was I?" Tom replied.

The staff member again glanced down at the pages on the clipboard. He had dropped the top pages so had to again lift them to find the previous day's list.

"Ah, here it is," he said, "according to this you attended, you've signed in as normal, is this your signature?" he asked turning the clipboard around for Tom to see the visitors list for the previous day.

Tom saw his signature, and nodded his acknowledgement, he then lifted his gaze to the top of the page which clearly showed the previous day and date.

The staff member could again see the confusion on Tom's face, and that he was struggling to comprehend the situation as it was unfolding before him. But there was nothing more he could do for him.

"Tom, why don't you go and speak to admin, see if they can make a phone call for you?"

Tom nodded at hearing that something had been said to him, although he had no idea of what had been said. He then slowly turned and walked back out of the visitor's wing, across the common area and the TV lounge where he had earlier waited, and eventually back to his room.

oOo

Once back in his room, Tom stripped off all of his outer clothes, which at this time of day consisted of the standard polo shirt and jogging trousers. There he stood in the middle of the floor, exposing all but for his underwear and socks. It was then that Tom made the discovery that he had missed earlier that morning. As he felt he was late for breakfast, he had rushed to get dressed, and in doing so had forgotten to check what he had made a conscious effort to check every morning for the last week or so. His underpants were now being correctly worn, not inside out as he was hoping they would be. This was the first time that this had happened since he had employed his totem to determine any infiltration by his alter-ego.

A totem is a sacred object or symbol that serves as an emblem of a group, clan or lineage. In this case to determine a constant or any variation of that constant.

As a result of this intervention, Tom had lost the whole of the previous day. But this wasn't just a day incarcerated in a secure hospital with no dealings other than that with fellow residents and staff, this intervention involved someone important to him, his friend and colleague Carl Wainwright.

Tom started to panic. What had been their interaction? Were there going to be consequences as a result of this missing day?

Once dressed again, Tom went to the administration office and asked if he could make a phone call to Carl. This was granted, and Tom watched tentatively as the clerk dialled the number held on file for Carl from behind the Georgian wire window.

Tom could feel his heart pounding itself out of his chest as he saw the clerk hold the phone to her ear. He could hear the ringing at the other end even from where he stood. It rang and rang. Eventually, it went to the pre-recorded voicemail message. The clerk then left a short message requesting a call back before hanging up.

She then spoke to Tom, "I'm sorry, no answer, I'll let you know when I get a reply."

Tom walked away disheartened and unnerved. He had lost a whole day, a day that could've involved anything. What *was* his interaction with Carl? Only time would now tell, Tom had to play the waiting game. Waiting to hear back from Carl.

oOo

The previous day Carl attended Yew Tree Hospital to visit Tom. Carl and Jess had entered into a rotation whereby they would visit on alternate weeks, so Tom only ever had to wait a week between visits.

Both Jess and Carl said they wanted to visit more often, but work commitments and the sheer distance needed to travel caused difficulties for them both. Tom had been at Yew Tree Hospital for almost three months now, so this had become a well-established routine.

After passing through the stringent security checks and having signed in, Carl was escorted through to the courtyard to meet with Tom.

On entering the courtyard, he could see a figure he recognised, he was sitting at a far table with his back towards him. Carl approached him. As he got close he placed a hand on his shoulder of the seated figure, which startled him. Carl could feel a sudden shudder beneath his hand. Carl saw him initially draw away from it before he turned to see Carl standing behind him. At first, his turning glance was aimed at chest height but was then elevated, passing over the name badge that Carl had been issued on his arrival. A smile then emerged over his face as a reaction to the gesture from his friend.

It was a smile that was only partially recognised, but Carl could easily forgive this, after all being in a place such as this did things to a person over time.

Carl still considered Tom to be a colleague as he had yet to be told anything to the contrary. He was still a warranted police officer, albeit one who had been sentenced to a course of indefinite medical treatment having been complicit to a series of brutal murders. But despite any of that, he was still a friend, and that's the reason he made this gargantuan journey every fortnight.

Carl circled around the other side of the table to face Tom. They exchanged smiles and Carl took a seat. This time Carl saw a more relaxed and familiar smile. He instantly deduced that the strained smile seen moments before was because his friend had turned to face the sun, causing him to squint.

He had sat with the morning sun to his back, so should Carl naturally take the chair opposite him, the sun would shine directly in his face. This would make for an uncomfortable arrangement, so Carl would most likely have to manoeuvre his seat.

Carl leant forward and put his hand on Tom's knee. "How's it going, buddy?"

But today it wasn't his *buddy* that was sitting next to him. Today it was Tomasz. But their personas had now become intertwined to such an extent that the mannerisms of each were being perfectly mimicked by the other making them virtually indistinguishable. Gone were the accents and personal attributes which identified each of them apart from the other.

Tomasz just smiled.

"That bad, eh?" Carl read into his lack of a verbalised response.

They both just sat there and exchanged blank glances for a few moments, neither knowing what to say to the other. Eventually, Carl thought of something to break the silence.

"Kilpatrick didn't pass the board, so he's been busted back down. He wasn't fucking happy, I can tell ya," Carl said.

Kilpatrick, their inspector, was in the position only on a temporary basis. But when he applied for the substantive position he failed to achieve the required standard, and as a result was reduced to his previous rank of detective sergeant, the same as Tom, only to have the senior position filled by another more suitable candidate.

Despite this being news that would have undoubtedly been the source of great amusement for them both in their office, it didn't get so much as a smile in return.

"I told ya that they've closed the books on Burgess, didn't I?" Carl couldn't recall if he had previously told Tom that their last investigation together had become exhausted, with all lines of enquiry followed as far as humanly possible. As a result, it had been filed pending any new information.

Tomasz just looked solemn. Carl was struggling to engage with him.

"Shame we couldn't kill two birds with one stone with that one," Carl started, "scum on scum crime shouldn't even be recorded; y'know, sometimes two wrongs *do* make a right."

Carl looked across at Tomasz. He noticed the slightest reaction from him, a tiny smile was starting to emerge on his face. Carl felt he was on to something, so he continued.

"You remember Parker, that scrotey little druggie down Westway?" Carl continued, "when he was stabbed up by the Kingsbury lot for selling on their patch?"

Carl knew full well that none of this would be news to Tom as he had led that investigation as much as he had led on the recently closed Burgess case. Carl was merely telling the story to entertain his friend. But his audience was not that of his friend.

"Well, we all knew who did it; Parker knew it, we knew, but remember we couldn't prove a bloody thing. Well, it's like you said at the time, *if we don't nip this in the bud now, this is gonna go mental,* or something like that, so we did what was necessary, didn't we? It was a fucking good idea of yours, too. Well, at the time it was anyway."

What *was* necessary? This started to have an intrigued reaction from Tomasz. His posture hadn't changed, but for the first time since Carl had sat down he had his full attention. In order to indulge Carl, he raised a fuller smile knowing that Carl would see this and carry on with his anecdote.

"You remember, we were on the verge of a turf war between those two gangs and it was gonna be an all-out cock fight if we didn't scare the shit out of them all. One lot encroaching on the other's patch, someone gets stabbed, so what was it you suggested doing then?" Carl paused to allow Tomasz to pick up the story from where he left it, but instead there was silence. Tomasz's gaze was to the ground, as if conjuring images to go with the narrative. After a few seconds, Carl took the hint to continue telling the story himself.

"You said that we needed to fit up the other gang, scare the shit out of them, they'd fuck right off out of it then, rather that, than hang around for anything to escalate. It was gonna get bloody, but you had the right idea."

Tomasz raised his gaze from the floor to look up in the blueness of the sky above them, and as he did a broader smile could be seen. As his eyes struggled with the brightness he closed them to allow his face to bask in the sunlight.

Carl, feeling he was on to a winner now continued to embellish.

"So, we sit down, over a pint, wasn't it? Down The Feathers if I remember rightly, and we decide who best to fit up; who, once fingered for the stabbing and out of the picture, is gonna rip the other gang apart, without him there'd be no gang, they'd be nothing, and they'd crawl away with their tails between their legs."

Carl chuckled, but still no complimenting reaction from Tomasz, though he appeared to be absorbing all of Carl's account as well as the sun.

"Then *you* pick the patsy, the fall guy, their leader, really the only one with any balls in their group, and we finger him. Didn't take much in the end, did it?"

Carl could see Tomasz's head slanting towards him, he could now see a look of interest, and maybe even joy in Tom's expression, so he continued.

"All it took was some carefully placed evidence, a little blood here, a weapon there... Fucking hell, TV taught us all we needed to know, didn't need all our fancy courses." Carl chuckled. "And given the history of hatred and rivalry between these two scumbags getting the charge for GBH wasn't difficult at all."

Carl looked over at the continued look of contentment in Tomasz's face.

"Then fucking Parker goes and fucking dies on us! I mean, what a tosser, fucks everything right up! Now we're dealing with a poxy manslaughter case, but the charge still sticks. Oh well, shit happens, I s'pose, he only served two years, but still it had the desired effect, the greater good and all that eh," Carl ended with a smile.

Carl looked across at Tomasz, he now looked oblivious to what had just been said, Carl now wondered if he had really heard a single word of it. If he had, he wasn't showing the sligntest reaction any more.

Then after a few seconds, Tomasz looked over towards Carl, looked at him with a stare that bore a hole right through him. Carl was the third victim of this stare, the first had been the custody sergeant when Tomasz had been charged following his arrest, the second was Jess in the visitor's centre of the prison at the end of their last visit before the trial, and now Carl.

"Shall we go for a walk?" Tomasz suggested as he put his hands on his knees and pushed himself to his feet, again in a manner indistinguishable from how Tom would've asked, and now with no discernible accent.

In an instant Carl felt uneasy. He didn't know who his audience was, he was no longer confident it was Tom he had been addressing. All he wanted was to be far away from him. The look he had been given scared him.

"Y'know what?" Carl said glancing down at his watch all too briefly to even register the time, "I do need to go, maybe next time eh?"

Carl was still sitting as Tomasz now towered over him, a complete role reversal to earlier, with Tomasz staring menacingly down on him. Tomasz deliberately stood directly between Carl's face and the sun, so he appeared enveloped in shadows and silhouettes, which only heightened Carl's fear.

Carl could feel his heart starting to race. He needed to get out of there and away from his friend as quickly as possible. In the confines of the space afforded him by Tomasz, he got to his feet and with great relief took a couple of large steps back to create a safe distance between the two of them.

Tomasz hadn't made any attempts to close down the distance between them. He just continued to look at Carl, however now without the accentuating effect of the sun behind him he appeared to be friendlier and less menacing. Carl started to doubt himself. Was he merely overreacting to a trick of the light? Surely, he was, after all this was Tom he was thinking about.

"Yeah, okay, next time then?" Tomasz said, "I'll see you in two weeks, yeah? Have a laugh at Kilpatrick for me, will ya?"

Carl nodded his acknowledgement to all that he'd just heard as he started walking backwards.

"Yeah, I'll see you soon," Carl replied as he turned and walked to the door entering the hospital wing. The last he saw of Tomasz was him waving as if seeing off a car full of people on a long journey.

Once alone again Tomasz sat back down.

There was rage building within him that had led to the suggestion to go for a walk. But there was an ulterior motive to suggesting the walk, one that would have undoubtedly ended their friendship.

It shouldn't have come as news to him, but it did. In an instant, everything he had come to believe was destroyed. Tom Draven was a bent copper, a copper that fabricated evidence to ensure a conviction.

It didn't matter whether Tom and Carl believed the guy they implicated may have committed the crime or not, it wasn't for them to decide. It was their job to investigate the crime and follow the evidence, not to decide who they felt did it and then ensure the evidence led to them. What if they were wrong, what if they ensured an innocent man had been convicted of the crime?

The man they ensured was convicted of the manslaughter charge did have a history of criminality, but that did not make him guilty of this offence.

Tomasz then began thinking about Pauline Barnes, Ronald Campbell and Leanne Young. In each case the evidence was there, beyond any doubt, that these people were guilty of the offence of which they were being investigated. All Tomasz had done was expedite the hand of law and pronounce judgement and sentence.

He then tried to justify to himself that perhaps falsely imprisoning someone for two years to avert a turf war between gangs was equally as justifiable as executing those guilty of their crimes. He couldn't. To him, what Tom and Carl had done was deplorable.

oOo

But Tom was not aware of any of this, he didn't know that Carl had revealed such details to Tomasz, and worse still the consequences that it may now have for him. Nothing made sense any more, all he knew was that this had to end.

DAY 185

The revelation of the previous week had taken a heavy toll on Tom. After realising that he had missed his visit with Carl he had felt a rage building within him, to such an extent that he felt that he was on the verge of losing control. This scared him, and as a result he knew he needed to take preventative steps himself. He felt the slightest adverse interaction could be the tipping point and cause the internal conflict he was suffering to erupt in a physical outburst. As a result, Tom had felt it best to isolate himself for the remainder of that day. He had returned to his room, and even boycotted the evening meal and kept himself to himself for everyone's benefit.

The more Tom thought about it the more he began to realise that it wasn't rage that was swelling within him, it was lust. A primal instinct to seek out and deliver retribution. It didn't seem to matter how he felt, whether he was calm and at peace, or active and focused, the lust was there, and it felt as if he were on the verge of it consuming him. For now, he felt it was he who was in control, but for how long?

In the following days his moods had swung like a metronome; one day he would be pleasant and loquacious, then the next he would again intentionally isolate himself and ignore any attempts from anyone to interact with him, be it from staff or residents.

oOo

Today, though, he felt fresher, more relaxed and more in control. He focused on having accepted the painful truth that he could no longer rely on who he believed himself to be. But there was one truth that Tom couldn't escape: that this situation he found himself in could not be allowed to continue.

After the debacle of the previous week's visitation it was good to have a visitor again, and better still for it to be Jess's turn.

"Have you heard from Carl at all," Tom asked as his first question after their greeting. He didn't even wait until he'd asked how Jess was herself.

"He mentioned that there was some mix-up last week, but that was about it, but he wouldn't elaborate on that," she replied.

Tom immediately felt that Jess wasn't being honest with him.

"He said he'd be back up when it was his turn again," she concluded.

Now Tom realised that she was lying to him.

Tom had been passed a message from Carl since his last visit in response to the phone message that had been left for him. He wanted Tom to know that he would not be visiting him any more, but that he wished him well. So why was Jess saying what she was?

oOo

In reality, Carl was on the phone to Jess as soon as he had got back into his car following his previous visit. "Jess, I'm literally on my way home from seeing Tom. I don't think the treatment's working. Can I come and see you?"

That evening the two of them met to discuss, not so much the apparent lack of progress in Tom's treatment, but that it was evident that he was regressing.

"By the end of the session I didn't feel it was him I was talking to at all," Carl said. "In hindsight, I don't think I should've discussed certain things with him, but the reaction I got genuinely scared me. I tell ya, I couldn't get out of there quickly enough."

"What did you regret telling him?" Jess enquired.

"Well, just to try and cheer him up, and, y'know, reminisce a bit I mentioned about previous cases we'd worked together," he paused reliving the moment for himself. "He then changed, like, in an instant. One second it was like he couldn't give a shit about anything, then the next he was glaring and menacing. I really thought he was gonna go for me."

"Carl," Jess replied, trying to make sense of the situation, "are you sure you're not reading too much into this? I mean, Tom's been through a lot, and what with the treatment, don't you think you're overreacting?"

"I wish I was Jess. Y'know I've got the greatest respect for Tom. But I mean it, he scared me, and I wouldn't be pressing the panic button if I didn't have genuine concerns." Carl paused to give full contemplation to what he had to say next. "I really don't think you should go and visit him any more… At least not 'til things have stabilised a bit, and until the treatment is progressing better. I just don't want what happened to me to happen to you, and I especially didn't want to keep this from you."

Time stood still for a moment, Carl looked at Jess as she was trying to make sense of it all. It was Jess who eventually broke the silence.

"I won't make a decision either way just yet, I've got a week to think about. But I will let you know what I decide, okay? I can't just turn my back on him."

Carl felt hurt by this remark, as if turning his back on Tom was what Jess considered he'd done.

oOo

Tom's question to Jess about Carl was expected, and she had rehearsed her response to it. But as this wasn't discussed with Carl she wasn't aware of his actions, that he had sent a message to Tom. Therefore, her response contradicted what he had in fact done, and what Tom knew to be a lie.

Although Tom knew what she had told him wasn't the truth, he had no intention of dwelling on it. At that moment in time, for all he knew she was trying to reassure him that his friend and colleague was looking forward to a future visit. Maybe he was, maybe he had reconsidered his decision after sending the message that Tom received?

Jess appeared calm and relaxed. She preferred the visits here as opposed to the prison, the freedom they had to interact allowed for them to escape the confines of the walls, and they could pretend they were anywhere but there. Even the coffee shop style table between them gave reference to past enjoyment.

They initially exchanged pleasantries with each other, but the small talk was soon exhausted, and the conversation then went on to the subject of Tom's treatment, and as a result, both his expression and mood distinctly changed. This subject disheartened him, and it didn't take long for his head to stoop and his shoulders to drop.

Tom looked across the courtyard. This time they weren't the only ones there. He wasn't happy with the fact that they may be overheard and suggested to Jess that they went for a walk.

"It's fine, really," she replied, "they're no more interested in us than we are in them."

But she could sense an ever-growing paranoia in Tom's attitude and demeanour, and she agreed to the walk in an attempt to pacify him.

As Tom stood he adjusted his joggers and straightened his shirt. In doing so a tobacco pouch fell from his pocket onto the floor between them. Tom hadn't seen it fall, but Jess did. At that point, she went to pick it up not knowing what it was. Returning to her seat she examined what she had retrieved.

"What's this?" Jess asked. "Have you started up again?"

As Tom was unaware of what he had dropped, Jess's response came as even more of a surprise. He looked at the item held prominently in her hand, then at the look on her face, and finally the words had meaning.

"It passes the time," came his reply. It was not something that Jess wanted to hear.

Reacting to her own disappointment, she tossed the tobacco pouch across the table at Tom, she was expecting him to catch it. But, he stood there unwavering, the pouch struck him in the chest and again fell to the ground without him making any effort to catch it.

She could see the disapproving look on his face and immediately attempted to rectify her lapse in judgement. "It really makes no difference to me," she said, "I'm just surprised is all."

As he crouched to reclaim his property from beneath the table, he muttered, "Jeśli to sprawia, że nie ma różnicy dla Ciebie, dlaczego się tak duża sprawa kurwa o tym?"

As he stood upright again he could see the confusion in Jess' expression. "What did you just say?" she asked.

"I said, if it makes no difference, why are you making such a big deal about it?"

Tom felt he should remove the sentiment of a *fucking big deal* from his rendition, assuming the profanity was what she had challenged him for.

"That's not what you said," she replied.

"Yes, it was." Tom protested. "What *did* I say then?"

"I don't know what you said," Jess stated, "I didn't understand a fucking word of it."

"How did you know what I did or didn't say then?" Tom said as he was pushing his chair under the table. Showing increasing agitation.

"Because it was in another fucking language, Tom. What the fuck is happening to you?"

Now the confusion was evident on Tom's face. To him, what he had just said was understood to him to be spoken in English, but Jess was adamant she had just heard him speak fluently in another language, most likely Polish.

"Tom, what *is* happening to you?" Jess asked again.

They were both in a state of shock, neither saying a word. The volume and emotion in their voices had increased as the conversation unfolded, and this had attracted the attention of the staff who were until then casually monitoring the courtyard, so they were now making conscious efforts to portray that everything was calm.

Tom took out his chair again and sat back down. He immediately sunk his head in his hands before drawing his fingers through his hair and clasping them behind his bowed head.

Jess rose to her feet and stepped around the table, she placed a single hand on top of Tom's clasped fingers.

Feeling her touch, he exploded into movement and rapidly jumped to his feet again, which sent his chair flying. His outthrust arms fell to his sides, which knocked her hand away. This made her jump and caused her to cry out in shocked surprise.

"Nie dotykaj mnie," he said.

Tom turned to face her. It was then that she saw the look that she had only ever seen once before. On that day, the last time she had visited with Tom in prison before his trial. That last time before he was led away into the corridor, before all hell broke loose. She never did find out what happened in that corridor, but it wasn't good.

That look scared her then, and it terrified her now. Similar to Carl reaction's the previous week. Jess had taken a few steps back in order to stand at a safe distance from Tom. She held her hands in prayer in front of her face, a look of terror in her eyes.

He looked down at his hands. His fists were clenched. His knuckles were white, and his hands were trembling. He could feel the rage coursing through him. He felt in control, but for how much longer?

Tom relaxed his hands and began to extend one towards Jess.

"Please," Jess said, "please don't touch me."

"I think you need to go," he said to her, "for your own good."

"I'm not going anywhere, I want to know what's going on? Carl *did* tell me what happened last week, he told me not to come here today. But I did, I chose to, I had to see it for myself, but he was right, something did happen! Please, Tom, what's happening to you?"

"I don't know, Jess, I just don't know... No one here seems to either. All I do know is that nothing seems to be working."

Tom looked around him, he saw that his chair had been knocked over by his efforts to stand up as quickly as he had. He stepped out and turned to pick it up. He then reset it by the table and again sat down.

"Do you want to go for a walk?" Tom asked.

Jess breathed a sigh of relief, his voice sounded calm. But, she didn't want to go for a walk. She didn't want to be anywhere but where they were. There were others who could come to her assistance if she needed them to. She too sat down to further affirm that their conversation needed to continue.

Until then they had commanded the attention of the courtyard. For Tom wanting privacy, not to have others listening in on their conversation, he had achieved just the opposite. But having seen both he and Jess retake their seats, the attention of the courtyard, including the staff, resumed to what it had been beforehand.

Tom now sat listing over to his right, with his right elbow on the armrest of his chair propping up his head, and his left hand in his lap.

"Nothing's working, Jess," Tom said, "I don't know what else there is that they can do. The worse thing is *they* don't have the first clue either. I'm being ripped open from the inside."

Jess was now clearly becoming more and more upset. She took two attempts to wipe away a tear. Once done she shuffled her chair around the side of the table. She knew she was putting herself at risk should Tom have another outburst, but she didn't care. This was the man she loved, and she wanted to be close to him.

The movement of the chair made more noise than she expected, and this again alerted the courtyard to their actions. Jess noticed a staff member paying them particular attention again.

Jess now sat at Tom's side. Hesitantly she extended a hand and placed it on top of the hand that Tom still had resting in his lap.

She was expecting a similar reaction to before, but she didn't care. She was prepared for an outburst, but this time, it didn't happen.

Tom's face was still resting on his other hand, she couldn't make out any expression. But after a few seconds, his hand had moved from under his cheek to cover both his eyes. It was then that his entire upper body started juddering, only to be followed by other indisputable signs that Tom was sobbing.

"It's okay, Tom, it's okay," she said, moving in closer and placing her arms around him, making her best efforts to comfort and console him.

Jess then looked up at the staff member who had again taken an interest in them. He had taken a couple of steps forward to improve his view of them. Jess looked at him, she shook her head to indicate that she was okay and didn't need any assistance from him. He nodded back and returned to his original position.

Tom had dropped the hand that was covering his face and buried his face in Jess's neck. He then pulled his hand out from underneath hers and held her close with both arms.

"Okay, everyone, time's up, can the visitors start making their way back inside?" the staff member announced whilst checking his watch. There was movement all around them, but neither Tom nor Jess reacted to the order in any way.

They hadn't moved in all the time the courtyard had taken to clear, and no one had given further suggestion that they should.

Eventually, Tom realised that he didn't want staff ending their moment together, so he must do it himself. Jess felt his movement so felt she had to reciprocate. As they came apart and their eyes adjusted to being open again they realised they were the only two people left in the courtyard now besides staff.

Jess paused, waiting for an action from Tom, when it didn't come she knew she had to act. She stood and looked down on him.

Still no reaction from him.

"Carl's no longer coming, so I will be next week, is that okay?" she asked.

There was still no reaction from Tom. Jess looked over at the staff member, who was beckoning her towards the doorway. She was now so far behind the other visitors that they were no longer in sight.

"I've got to go now, sweetie," she said as she leaned forward and kissed him gently on the top of his head.

Tom then extended a hand towards her, which she took. She was expecting this to bring Tom to his feet, but he didn't move beyond his gesture. Knowing the onus was on her to move, she stepped back which caused their grips to fail and their arms to fall to their sides.

Jess took a couple of steps back. "I'll see you next week," she said as she turned and walked towards the door. She took one last glance back at Tom who had turned slightly towards her.

She smiled.

DAY 186

Tom started the next day doing his utmost to avoid any personal contact with either staff or residents. Not only did he miss his breakfast, but he didn't even leave his room until after staff had attended there to check on him.

When he did eventually emerge, he sat alone during lunch, and afterwards he was again seen to sit alone in the communal area. He was reading the final few pages of the novel that he had been seen with over the last couple of weeks. He wore his spectacles low on his nose, so he also had focus on the rest of the room.

His days now cycled through the same sequence of events. They consisted of nothing more than reading, walking the grounds, smoking and occasionally eating. Just before lunch he had been reading, before going outside for a cigarette.

Having gone outside to smoke, he had tucked his book and his tobacco pouch under his arms in order to leave his hands free to roll a cigarette. As he raised the rolled cigarette to his mouth to moisten the paper to adhere it to itself, he inadvertently dropped his tobacco pouch and his book on the grass. In his reaction to catch the falling items he dropped the unfinished cigarette. The pouch opened as it fell, and this caused the tobacco to spill out onto the grass, and the book fell open at a page. This was seen by a member of staff who felt he had a duty to inspect the tobacco to ensure it wasn't tainted in any way.

As the staff member arrived on the scene he saw that Tom was on his knees, and already in the process of brushing leaf debris from the pages of his book before sweeping the tobacco back into its pouch.

"Surely you're not gonna smoke that?" came the inevitable question.

"It's fine," Tom replied as he was rummaging around in the tobacco and picking out the occasional piece of dirt, blade of grass or twig.

When the staff member protested, exclaiming how anyone could possibly want to smoke such a concoction he merely replied, "Pads it out a bit, makes it last longer."

The staff member could see a bizarre logic in this reply. He had fulfilled his responsibility, ensuring that no foreign bodies that could actually cause Tom any harm were left in the tobacco, and as result allowed Tom to continue in his task.

Once he had cleared up what was left of the tobacco he put the pouch back in his pocket without having actually rolled a cigarette.

This appeared bizarre to the staff member, but he just put this down to his intervention, and that maybe his involvement had distracted Tom beyond his desire to smoke at that time.

oOo

Tom could expect a hypnotherapy session that afternoon, but until he was called for it he had to entertain himself. So, after lunch, he again frequented the communal area and found the same space on the sofa where he had been sitting that morning. He carried on reading from where he had left off that morning.

After a while, he looked up from his book, took his spectacles off and rubbed the back of his hand across his eyes. He looked at the clock, they should've called him for his session by now, but still nothing. He guessed they would call for him when the session was ready, evidently just not yet.

He looked outside and saw what a glorious afternoon it was.

He got up from his chair and walked across the sparsely populated communal area. As it was such a lovely day he thought that most of the residents were perhaps enjoying the grounds or had visitors.

Once outside, whilst on the paved area immediately outside of the door, he took off his spectacles and using the same arm wiped his brow with the back of his forearm. This knocked the spectacles from his grasp, causing them to fall. They bounced off his shoe before hitting the ground which made them shoot forward a few feet. Tom stepped after them to retrieve them.

Having bent down to pick them up the same staff member who had seen Tom drop his tobacco pouch earlier that morning came over to speak to him. "Not having a good day are you, Tom?" he said. "Have you broken them?"

The staff member looked at the ground immediately beside his feet, he could see what appeared to be fresh scratch marks on the paving slab. The staff member then beckoned to him to hand over the spectacles for inspection. "Let me see them please, Tom," he asked.

Once handed the spectacles he inspected them and he could see no damage at all, and certainly no abrasion damage which could have caused the gouges to the paving slab.

At that moment, his radio crackled to life, it was a message requesting urgent assistance elsewhere in the hospital.

Satisfied that there wasn't any damage to the spectacles he handed them back. "Tom, you've gotta be more careful with these things y'know," he said as he hurried back inside the building.

He didn't get a word in reply.

That afternoon's therapy session was cut short by the hypnotherapist as his subject was being uncooperative and obstructive throughout the process.

"I can't work miracles all by myself," the hypnotherapist said towards the premature end of the session, "if you're not prepared to work with me, Tom, there's no point in either of us being here."

The hypnotherapist looked at Tom expecting a response, Tom had never intentionally been rude throughout any of their previous sessions. The hypnotherapist had conducted the entire session believing that it was Tom who was the subject. But now he wasn't so sure and attempted to obtain clarification before the session ended.

"Tom, is it you I am talking to?" came the question. He was expecting a verbalised response as per the norm from the polite and courteous Tom. But no response was forthcoming. This left the hypnotherapist bewildered and concerned.

The session, to that point had been structured around the belief that it was Tom who was the subject. Where ideas, dreams and character traits were encouraged to flourish. Had he realised that the subject was in fact Tomasz, in line with previous sessions any responses would be played down in an attempt to subdue them.

With the subject having now left the treatment room the hypnotherapist was left alone. He began hastily scribbling his notes, reviewing the session and outlining possible outcomes due to his oversight.

oOo

That evening after dinner, staff could see Tom sitting outside alone rolling a cigarette, on one of the benches next to the paved area where he had earlier dropped his spectacles and lit the cigarette. It was getting late, but he was determined to enjoy it before time was called and the residents then being required to go to their rooms.

In the fading light, it hadn't been noticed that he was still wearing his spectacles. This was an oversight on the part of the staff, as breakable personal items such as spectacles should not be taken outside. It may have been brought up earlier as Tom was wearing them when he spilt his tobacco, had the staff member not have been required to depart so abruptly, responding to urgent assistance required elsewhere in the hospital.

A few minutes after the first cigarette had been finished he began to notice that it was becoming chilly. So, he got up from the bench and went back towards the doors leading to the communal area.

It was then that a staff member noticed his spectacles.

"You know you shouldn't have those outside, Tom?" came the rhetorical question.

"Well isn't that down to you guys to take them from me," came the insolent reply, "I had 'em outside with me earlier on and nothing was said then."

"I don't care what happened *earlier,* I wasn't working *earlier*. Come on, hand 'em over and you can go back to your smoking," demanded the staff member.

He slipped them from his nose, blinked a few times to allow his vision to adjust before holding them out for the staff member to take. Having approached where he stood the staff member inspected the spectacles to ensure they were all in order with no damage, as per the reason for the policy before folding them and gently putting them in the breast pocket of his shirt. Once satisfied the staff member turned and walked away. He turned back briefly to look at Tom, as he went back outside to continue smoking.

The foreign debris that had been collected in with the tobacco earlier that day was now causing him to cough intermittently as he smoked it. He took the cigarette from his mouth and examined it.

As he continued to smoke the coughing became uncontrollable. He couldn't understand why. He took the cigarette from his mouth and examined it, he shrugged his shoulders before putting it back in his mouth and taking another puff. As he did so, he took the tobacco pouch from his pocket. He opened it, prodded the contents with his fingers, and stirred it around to examine it. He could clearly see that it had become tainted. Foreign debris had got caught up with the tobacco.

It was this that was most likely causing him to cough. He weighed up the options of either smoking tainted tobacco or not smoking at all, and having decided on the outcome he shrugged his shoulders again and took a long drag from the cigarette, finishing it off, before flicking the butt away. He watched the crescendo of smoke and glowing ash fly in an arc from his fingers onto the lawn.

From his position near the doors to the communal area he was able to see the clock inside on the wall, it read 9:35 p.m. There was more than enough time to try to enjoy one more cigarette, tainted or not, before being made to turn in. *What else was there to do?* he thought.

Within seconds another expertly rolled cigarette found its way between his lips and was lit. He saw no point in returning to the bench, so leaned back against the wall and enjoyed the view of the twilight lit grounds ahead of him.

As he was so adept at rolling cigarettes now, since the loss of his rolling machine, he rolled a third cigarette as he enjoyed the second. This was done with the intention of having one ready for the morning. Or he may have a sneaky one during the night should he wake, either way he was prepared.

"Okay, gentlemen, time please," came a voice from within the communal area. Was it his intention perhaps to sound like a pub landlord, as opposed to a staff member at a hospital for the criminally insane sending the afflicted to their rooms for the night? Either way, it got the desired response without so much as an objection from any of the residents. Slowly they vacated the communal area to go back to their rooms, rooms where anyone can enter during the night, but the residents can't exit until released the following morning.

oOo

Once in his room, he prepared for bed much as he had since establishing his totem, where he would go to sleep naked and wake, and intentionally wear his underpants inside out in order to determine whether or not he had become his alter-ego in the interim.

So far Tom was confident it was working. Only on one occasion, since the day he met with Director Waldwin and established this routine, did Tom have to rely on his totem. That was following the day that he missed his visit with Carl.

He spent quite some time after the enforced 'lights out' sitting on a chair staring out of the window. His window didn't share the same glorious view he had enjoyed earlier in the day, no view at all in fact as the glass was frosted, but he wasn't really looking at the view. He was imagining the world, and the lives beyond it, and realising that his being in this hospital was the final chapter in the saga that brought him here.

As he sat, he ran his tongue across his teeth and tasted the burnt tobacco on them. He looked across at the tobacco pouch that was now sitting on the table beside the bed. He contemplated having that pre-rolled cigarette he made surplus to his requirements earlier, but then thought better of it. He wasn't feeling all that good; was it the lack of sustenance that day or was it just because he felt so confused about recent events, and possibly disillusioned by the apparent lack of progress in his treatment?

Finally, he decided it was time to lie down. He lay flat on his back with his arms under the covers, and after a couple more, short coughing fits he closed his eyes.

DAY 187

The next morning started the same as the previous day.

Tom had again failed to attend breakfast, but because a pattern was emerging it was not deemed necessary for staff to attend his room with any great sense of urgency.

Eventually, a member of staff was sent. He knocked and waited and knocked and waited. Eventually, on getting no reply, he entered Tom's room.

Tom was seen to be still lying in bed, the covers were drawn up to his chin. His arms beneath the covers. He looked asleep, perfectly at peace.

"C'mon, Tom," the staff member said, "time to wake up. If you don't hurry you'll miss breakfast."

There was no reply and still no movement.

"Tom, come on, wake up, you're making me look bad."

Still nothing.

"All right, Tom, have it your way but I ain't coming over there," he said, and then called into his radio, "yeah, can I get some assistance down at A23, he's playing silly buggers?"

"Right, Tom, that's help coming, are you gonna get yourself up now, or are we gonna 'ave to do it for you?" He paused. "Now what's it gonna be?"

Within minutes, two other staff members, one of which was Malcolm, appeared in the doorway.

Malcolm smiled gleefully, hoping that today would be the day he would be able to have some fun at Tom's expense.

The first staff member approached the nearside of the bed. The other two positioned themselves around the bed should Tom decide to play up in any way.

"Ready?" said the first staff member as he took a good grip of the bedding. Malcolm had taken an identical hold opposite him. He nodded to acknowledge his readiness. In one swift movement, they both stripped the bed of the sheets and the charcoal coloured blanket.

All three then looked down at Tom in horror.

Tom lay dead in the bed.

Epilogue

That morning, when Tom had failed to attend breakfast as expected and staff members entered his room and found him lying dead in his bed, the sheets and mattress were soaked with blood. Yet no trauma or any signs of a struggle was immediately apparent.

Tom's room was sealed off, and only after it was ruled out that any other person was involved was Tom's body removed, initially to the infirmary, before being taken to the mortuary of the nearest hospital.

Once the body had been removed, a thorough search of the room was able to take place. During this search, a single piece of folded paper was found under the pillow. It appeared to be a page torn from a novel, yet there was no printing on it. The page contained a handwritten note.

Also, beneath the pillow, a short piece of metal was found, it was about two inches in length.

When it was examined it had been sharpened to a point. This was deemed consistent to have been done using a coarse stone, or by dragging it along a paving slab or brickwork.

During the autopsy on Tom's body, it became apparent that puncture wounds had been caused to the inside of both wrists, in turn, piercing major blood vessels. This caused the massive loss of blood as seen on the bed sheets, to such an extent that after his body was removed it was found that a sizeable pool of blood had collected on the mattress and that droplets were also found on the floor below. This was not readily apparent when Malcolm and the other staff members entered Tom's room because of the charcoal coloured blanket that formed the top layer of bedding.

Following the autopsy and inquest, the cause of death was stated to be inconclusive. This was deemed the appropriate verdict as no single cause of death could be determined. It was stated that Draven had died of exsanguination (severe loss of blood), but equally, he showed evidence of being poisoned. With either method equally having possibly proven fatal, neither could be determined as the cause of death.

The poison was identified as being derived from the *Taxus Bacccata,* more commonly known as the yew tree.

It was later determined that the means by which the toxins were introduced into Draven's body was by aspiration, specifically that he had inhaled the toxic vapours having smoked the leaves and/or berry seeds of the yew tree along with his tobacco. The source of the poisoning was proven from an analysis of the remaining tobacco found in his room.

Furthermore, it was proven that the novel that Tom had been reading had been used to secrete and desiccate the yew tree leaves over a period of time. It was concluded that he had done this to prepare the leaves to be later included in the tobacco pouch. The same novel was also found to be the origin of the page used to write the note found under the pillow.

The implement used to cause the puncture wounds was determined to be the same two-inch-long piece of metal that had been found beneath Tom's pillow along with the note. It originally had been part of Tom's spectacles and had been detached and sharpened to a point at one end. The missing piece was not immediately apparent on casual inspection of the spectacles, as it would normally have been hidden beneath a plastic covering.

During Tom's studies as part of his criminology degree at university, he had reason to research the case of Doctor Hawley Harvey Crippen (11/9/1862 – 23/11/1910). Crippen was hanged for the murder of his wife Cora Henrietta Crippen (née Turner) at Pentonville Prison, London on the 23rd November 1910.

After his conviction and being sentenced to death, Crippen's aim was to cheat the hangman by using a detached piece of his spectacles to puncture a vein so as to bleed out whilst he slept during the night before his execution. However, the spectacles were seen by his guards to have a piece missing. A thorough search was conducted which located the missing piece on him – thus foiling his plans. He was hanged the next day.

Less commonly known was the toxic effects of yew tree leaves and the seeds of the berries on the human body. This was something that Tom was only aware of having dealt with a suicide by identical means a few years earlier where it was only identified as the cause of death by an admission from the deceased on the suicide note.

But why would Tom need to double up on the efforts to kill himself? Well, he didn't.

Tom had planned to poison Tomasz, knowing Tomasz would continue smoking the tobacco blissfully unaware that it was tainted. As a result, any suffering would be incurred solely by Tomasz. Although they occupied the same body, Tom would be dormant, and although his life would end, he wouldn't suffer or even be aware it had taken place, much like he had gone to sleep on many a night previously only to wake up as Tomasz. Tom felt he needed to do this because all therapeutic efforts to quell the monster within him had failed. He felt he had no choice and that time was running out. He felt he was less and less in control as time went on.

Tomasz, on the other hand, felt that Tom needed to be punished for being a corrupt cop, after both he and Carl had fabricated evidence to secure a conviction on Tom's suggestion. He chose to punish him by imposing the same sentence as he had done on Campbell and Barnes, and it was Tomasz, realising his own sacrifice, who punctured his own veins knowing that as a result Tom would never wake again.

With no discernible cause of death, it will forever remain a mystery as to who exacted their vengeance on the other.

The note was analysed. The handwriting in part matched that of Tom after having been compared to police reports that he had made, and also to the list of historical investigations that he had been involved with that had been seized into evidence prior to his arrest. However, it was determined that the note contained content written by two different hands, the second being a perfect mirror image of the first. This was compared in style and pressure to the police reports that Tomasz signed whilst in custody and doodles made by him in court during the trial.

The content of the note written by Tom made an apology to all those who knew and loved him. Tom stated that he felt he was succumbing to his demon and was losing ever more control on a daily basis, and that he couldn't allow this cold-blooded killer to destroy him too. The interspersed content written by Tomasz made an allegation to the chief officer of Tom's force claiming that both Tom Draven and Carl Wainwright were implicit in fabricating evidence in the case of Christopher Parker and that an innocent man was currently languishing in prison. The letter also stated that Wainwright had confessed this to him implicating Draven, and as a result he found Draven guilty.

Based on this letter, DC Wainwright is currently suspended from duty and is the subject of internal and criminal investigations. The case of manslaughter against Christopher Parker is currently under review.

Jess was shown a sanitised copy of the letter, as Tom's last words spoke fondly of her and said a regrettable goodbye. Despite her best efforts, she was denied access to the original note.

The case into the murder of Callum Burgess remains unsolved.

The End

Also by John T. Leonard:

A Life's Work (published with Pegasus)

Settling the Score

The Second Wrong

The Hunted: Heart of a Lion – Part 1

The Hunted: Heart of a Lion – Part 2

Vindicated